The Signet

BEN SWENSON

PAGE PUBLISHING, INC.
New York, NY

First originally published by Page Publishing, Inc. 2018

The Signet is a work of fiction. Apart from well-known actual events and various locations that play into the story line, all names, characters, places, and incidents are fictitious and the product of the author's imagination.

ISBN 978-1-64424-166-0 (Paperback)
ISBN 978-1-64424-167-7 (Digital)

Printed in the United States of America

CONJECTURE

Sometimes things fall apart so that
better things can fall together.
—Marilyn Monroe, 1926–1962

Many people are not fully knowledgeable of the signet ring, though it has existed for centuries. Typically, it was a finger ring with a flat bezel upon which the wearer's official seal, name, symbol or family crest, known as the chop, were engraved. Signet rings, normally worn by royalty, people of authority or of great wealth, were used to seal an important missive by pressing the ring's chop into the warm sealing wax. This sealed the document, prevented tampering, and identified the sender.

Throughout history, jewelry—particularly that which is beautiful in design, small in size, and made of precious metals—were prized possessions. As such, small items of worth were considered spoils of war by soldiers of invading armies—taken by force and sent home to mothers and/or other family members (a very common practice by Japanese soldiers ravaging Chinese cities and the surrounding areas during the 1930s). Again, such "souvenirs" were often held for years by a Japanese family until, many years later, some family member with no real knowledge of or any attachment to the item sold it for its karat weight value.

In April of 1994, a signet ring of this type was noticed in a Tokyo boutique that dealt in high-end Oriental antiques. After negotiating a price, it was purchased by a young American then in Japan on business. What little was known of the ring's origin had been revealed by an artisan's logo still faintly discernable inside the ring's band. Such markings are similar to a mintmark on a coin and can often assist in determining age and place of origin. This ring was determined to be Chinese in origin and crafted by a well-known and highly skilled goldsmith who lived near the city of Tientsin during the late 1700s. The chop engraved on the bezel of the ring was identified as a Chinese character with duel interpretation, meaning either good fortune or long life. The ring's presence in Japan after more than two hundred years, along with other pertinent history, is open to conjecture.

PREFACE

Knowledge beyond that of an
adversary is power undisplayed.
—Confucius, 551–479 BC

In the course of living history, almost everyone will have experienced something strange, maybe almost supernatural, for which there is no explanation. As an example, an elderly couple is driving across the country when the wife becomes suddenly ill and tells her husband she really needs medical assistance. As quickly as possible, he leaves the highway at the next exit indicating a small town and drives directly to a medical facility, where his wife receives the necessary medical treatment. It isn't until much later that it dawns on the husband that he had never been in that town before but had known exactly where to go for medical help. At such times, some will wonder and try to rationalize what happened, while others will just accept the fact that there is no answer, put the matter behind them, and get on with their lives.

On the evening of July 7, 1942, one month after the Battle of Midway Island, America's first clear-cut victory in the Pacific, an American sailor home on shore leave while his ship was undergoing repairs at the Bremerton Naval Shipyard walked toward a Chinese restaurant in the south end of Seattle, Washington. Painted in large gold-colored letters above the entrance was the name Golden Pheasant, faintly visible in the approaching darkness.

Tossing his cigarette into the gutter, he crossed the street and entered the building, where he was greeted by a young Chinese man. "Good evening, sir. Are you here for dinner?"

Looking around, the sailor said, "I'd like to talk to the Chinaman."

In a low voice, the waiter asked, "What is it you want, sir?"

Clearly uncomfortable, the sailor lit a cigarette, took a drag, and said, "I've been told if a person wishes to place a large wager on something, he should come here and ask to talk to the Chinaman."

"Oh, yes, I understand. Please follow me."

Butting his smoke in an ashtray, the sailor quickly followed and was led through the kitchen to a small office in the rear of the building.

Pointing to one of two chairs adjacent to a long, narrow table, the waiter nodded and said "Please be seated" and left. ·

Looking around, the sailor sized up the room. Beside the table and chairs, the only other object in the room was a large wooden roll-top desk. The floor was carpeted, and the faint smell of incense was in the air. No sound of any kind could be detected. After a short wait that seemed like hours, an elderly Chinese gentleman quietly entered and sat across the table from the sailor. Dressed in a black padded silk gown and a silk skullcap, he wordlessly appraised the young sailor. The waiter reentered the room with a tea service, sat it on the table, and left as quietly as he appeared. Pouring tea into two cups, the elderly gentleman moved to his visitor's side of the table, leaning back into his chair. Smiling, he said, "I am Mr. Wu. People have been known to call me the Chinaman. How can I be of service to you?"

Shifting forward to the front edge of his chair and taking a deep breath, the sailor said, "I want to make two large wagers, and I've been told you might be the person to talk to."

Sipping his tea, Mr. Wu looked intently at his visitor and replied, "I've been known to put money at risk. What is it you wish to wager on?"

Ignoring the cup of tea at his elbow, the sailor continued, "I want to bet that we'll beat Germany and on what date they will surrender unconditionally and, if I win, bet the whole bundle on what date Japan will surrender unconditionally."

Placing his teacup upon the tea service, Mr. Wu looked at the ceiling and asked, "How much do you wish to wager?"

Taking a drink of his now-lukewarm tea, the sailor sat back in his chair and said, "All I got—$2,300. And I want big odds." As they looked at each other, the room again became very quiet.

"As a member of the US Navy, you realize these are uncertain times," said Mr. Wu. "What if, excuse me, but this must be considered? What if you meet with unfortunate circumstances?"

Smiling, the sailor replied, "Then, Mr. Wu, it's all yours—all of it, win, lose, or draw."

Standing, Mr. Wu bowed his head and said, "In my homeland, it is believed that a man who is willing to be put at risk shall be favored by the gods. We shall see whose joss is supreme. Come dine with me, and we shall solidify our wager agreement."

With this meeting, information gained in a manner not believable or explainable set in motion the fickle wheels of fortune that would not culminate until far in the future.

INDECISION

When in doubt, don't take
a knife to a gunfight.
—Wyatt Earp, 1848–1929

Huntington Beach, California
May 1994

As a kid, my mother called me a dreamer. As an adult, I'm a dreamer, but only when I have the time to be. Today I have the time. My name is Wes Jenner, and having just returned from a business trip the previous evening, I really need to unwind. The trip had included several Pacific Rim countries and culminated in Japan. Big sales presentations, back-to-back, took their toll. I'm going to sleep the weekend away and recuperate. Thinking back over the last couple of days, I can't help but think that thirteen hours of flight time from Japan is not a fun trip for a guy my size, even in first class. I must be getting too old for this business.

Stepping out onto the sundeck, I can feel the warmth of the morning sun and taste the salt air. Standing at the rail, I watch the same old Saturday morning routine: joggers running along the beach path. To the north, oil wells—looking dinosaurian as they bob up and down—constantly pull oil from deep below the seabed. As I look westward out on the horizon, a lone Navy destroyer makes its way south to San Diego. Closer ashore, a bunch of surfers, like a group of ducks, float about waiting for that right wave. As I gaze at the beach, I can't help but think that I'm just like those surfers—just marking time waiting for something right to happen.

Nursing a cup of lukewarm coffee, I look at the pile of mail that has accumulated during my three-week absence. Stretching gingerly, I pull the box of collected correspondence over to the small sundeck table and sit down. Absentmindedly, I start sorting through the pile of envelopes, tossing the junk mail in the trash can by my left foot and bills in a pile by my right. Contest envelopes are set aside, thinking maybe I might get lucky. The beige envelope stops me in midmotion. Even after two years, the tiny script writing with large loops is easy to recognize. "Damn it, Pam, please get the hell out of my life." Muttering to myself, I contemplate throwing it in the trash. The letter is postmarked San Francisco and dated two weeks earlier. Knowing that I'd read the damned thing anyway, I tear the flap with my thumb and remove a single sheet of paper.

After rereading the letter one more time, I stand, crumple the letter into a ball, and slam-dunk it into the trash can. Walking into the kitchen, I grab a can of Coors from the refrigerator and then, stepping into the living area, survey the room. Boxes of books, dishes, pictures, and God only knows what else sit untouched where they were placed two years ago. "Wesley, old man," talking to the guy in the mirror, I said, "all you have here is a junkyard and a place to sleep between business trips. It's time for you to put your butt in gear and get a life."

Monday morning, the drive from the beach to my office in Irvine seems different. The day seems brighter, the traffic lighter, and even the coffee and donut consumed during the drive seem better than usual. Waving at the front office staff, I head down the hall toward the sales office. Stopping at the receptionist's desk, I hand her a small package before she can utter a word. "Mr. Jenner, welcome home. What is this?"

"Just something for you, Carrie. I thought you might like it." I watch as she unwraps the package, revealing a delicate small cloisonné vase.

"Wesley—uhh . . . Mr. Jenner—oh, this is so beautiful. Thank you. Thank you so much." Giving her a wink, I head on down the hall to my office. Upon entering, I stop and look around. Oh yeah, nothing has changed: neat, clean, utilitarian, devoid of any personal stuff. Neat and clean was Carrie's doing.

Utilitarian, reflecting my lifestyle of the past two years. As I set my briefcase on my desk, a welltailored tall man enters the office.

"Hey, Wes, welcome home, buddy. Man, you did a fantastic job!"

I turn and, smiling, say, "Hi, Charley. It's good to be back. By the way, I quit."

Charles Dunning Madden is senior VP of sales at California Machine and Milling, known in trade circles as CalMac. The company is currently riding the crest of a fantastic sales year, driven mostly by my foreign sales. It doesn't take a PhD in psychology for Charley to realize he has a big problem in the making. He can tell I'm dead serious. "Whoa. That's a hell of a way to say hello. Are you serious or what?"

With a smile, I reply, "Yeah, Charley, I am."

Stepping to the doorway, Charles Madden motions to the receptionist. "Carrie, would you be kind enough to get us coffee, please?" Turning back into the room, he pulls up a chair. Straddling it, he sits down and asks, "Okay, buddy, what's going on? What happened? You walked out of here a month ago ready to take on the world. Singapore sales were more than the company expected. Then the Japanese sales figures were totally unbelievable. The production and training people are hard-pressed to meet scheduled delivery time frames. Hell, at the directors' meeting last Thursday, the talk was centered on giving you everything west of the Mississippi River as well as Canada to boot. Now this morning, you walk in here, and the first thing out of your mouth is 'Hi, Charley, I quit.' Dammit, Wes, you owe me more than that."

Entering the room carrying a tray of coffee and cups, Carrie sneaks a wink at me as she sets the tray on the desk. Turning to leave, Charley asks her to tell his secretary where he is. "Tell her also that we're not to be disturbed, please."

Pouring coffee, I realize that it has been a hell of a way to greet my boss. Three years ago, I had been a junior engineer working in the research and development lab perfecting microminiature milling machines, producing fine finishes on metal parts unsurpassed by any equipment then available. Charles Madden, tasked with expanding the overseas markets, needed someone who was technically familiar as well as proficient in presenting their product to potential customers. He had selected me over several other engineers thought to be more qualified for the task at hand. His choice had proved to be correct. Charley may be a clotheshorse, but he could always spot talent. Within a year, my sales record was above and beyond that of my peers at CalMac.

"I'm sorry, Charley. You're right. I do owe you more than that. I owe you everything. I am sorry, really. I got into LAX late Friday night, and I've had all weekend to sit and think. You know, Charley, for three years, all I've lived for is this job. Two years ago, my wife left me—ran off with some forest ranger in a Smokey the Bear hat. Left me to go up and live in the woods somewhere. Who knows, maybe if I had been home more, that wouldn't have happened. I don't know. Charley, I'm not pointing fingers, really. I just don't see any light at the end of the tunnel. I've got no personal life—nothing. Hell, a big night for me is going down to the local sports bar and beating all the locals at Sports Trivia. I've got to get away and get my head on straight."

Rising from the desk with coffee cup in hand, I walk to the window where I can see the sun reflecting off the windshield of my Benz. Turning and looking at Charley, "I bought a car, a place on the beach, and now it's just beginning to dawn on me: I'm just running and trying to hide from myself." Looking Charley eye to eye, I decide, to hell with it. Let it all hang out. "When I got back from this trip, there was a letter waiting for me from Pam. She's going to visit her sister in LA later this week. She wants to meet with me."

Charley refills his coffee cup. "Oh, yeah." He thinks to himself. He remembers Pamela well. The poor man's Ava Gardner. Young, built like a Greek goddess, and shoulder-length dark hair that just glistens in the sun. A country girl completely out of her element in an urban setting.

Taking a cigarette out of a silver case and then remembering that I don't smoke, he doesn't light it but points it at me and says, "She would have left regardless. She wanted something you were not ready to give her: country, dogs, and kids. Your problem, pal, is that you are just too damned easy. You're like a cafeteria: charge for a cup of coffee and give away the refills. She walked out while you were on a trip and took damned near everything you had. Then you gave her half of everything that was left when you got back. Now she's coming back for another bite of the apple."

Seeing the hurt in my eyes, Charley quickly backs down. Moving quickly to where I'm standing, he puts a hand on my shoulder and says, "Look, it's my turn to apologize. I had no right to say what I did. I'm sorry, really. You're a nice guy, Wes, and you deserved a lot more than what you got. Look, I think I can see where you're coming from. Don't do anything rash just yet. Take care of your paperwork, tie up all the loose ends, and we can talk this matter out later, okay?" I just nod as Charley walks out of the room.

Several hours later, having cleared the office paperwork, travel vouchers, and accumulated correspondence, I take off down the hall for the office coffee lounge, actually feeling good about what has transpired with Charley. Charley is a straight shooter, and right, wrong, or indifferent, he says what he believes and lets the chips fall where they may.

Passing Carrie's desk, I see the small vase with a single rose sitting in a prominent place and get a smile and another thanks as I pass by. I know that I can do no wrong in her eyes. I'm the son she never had. She looks out for me like a mother hen or, better yet, like El Toro: screw with the bull and you'll get the horn!

Entering the lounge, I see my aerospace counterpart inspecting a large box of donuts. "Okay, George, leave a jelly-filled for me."

Grinning, the man turns and says, "Hey, Ace, welcome back. How was the sushi? The word is out that you sold everything except the office furniture. Wanna trade territories?"

"Oh, sure, George. Why didn't you make that offer when aerospace was still booming?" Laughing, George shoots me a gesture and walks out the door.

Walking down the hall with my fourth cup of coffee of the day, I approach Charley's office. His secretary looks up and smiles. "Hello, Wesley. I hear that you're quite a souvenir hunter." Winking, she motions me to go in. As I walk by, I can't help but sneak a peek at the greatest set of legs in the building.

As I enter, Charley is just hanging up his phone. "Come on in and shut the door so we can have some privacy. Well, you sure have made it tough for the rest of the sales guys. Every woman in the building has heard about Carrie's cloisonné vase. What's the matter, you couldn't find a box of chocolates?"

I just grin and hold out my hand to display a very large and ornate gold signet ring. "They made the vase part of the deal if I bought the ring. It's supposed to bring me good luck."

Charley looks at the ring and shakes his head. "Man, there's enough gold there to make a barbell. You're going to get tired just packing it around. Come on and sit down. I've had several conversations with the board of directors and the CEO so far this morning. Bottom line, they don't want to lose you, and from a personal standpoint, I don't want to see you walk away either. I could be wrong, but I know you had a rough trip and you are making a snap decision. Don't go off half-cocked. I want you to give it some deep thought, okay?

Nodding, I take a sip of coffee, waiting for Charley to continue. Walking across the room and adjusting some family pictures sitting on the bookcase, Charley turns and says, "I have three things for you to consider: First, you need some time to get your personal life back on track. Second, you haven't taken any time off in three years. You need a vacation. Third, while you were away this past month, representatives from a large Canadian manufacturing firm visited our facilities and expressed great interest in our microfinish applications to possibly correct problems unique to their business. They will be meeting with all their subsidiaries in Vancouver next month. They have asked us to be represented. However, there's one big caveat. Are you ready for this? CalMac wants you there, and dammit, Wes, I want you there also. You put together everything you need to investigate their needs and, if a feasible application exists, present and demonstrate the capabilities of our product. Both the shipping department and engineering personnel will ensure everything you deem necessary is there, up and running, as you determine your needs. It will be basically the same as the Japanese package: sales, service, and training. Repeat the Japanese deal with the Canadian firm, and I promise you a bonus like you've never seen. But regardless of how it goes or whatever you decide to do, I'll back you 100 percent."

I stand, nod to Charley, and shake his hand. Then, taking my coffee cup, I leave the office.

4

COMMITMENT

Damn, try for the high ground.
—George Armstrong Custer, 1839–1876

Huntington Beach, California
One week later

Sitting on my sundeck, I wiggle in the lounge chair with my hands clutched behind my head, watching the surfers. The tide is out and the water still. Mothers with small children are scattered along the water's edge. Yawning, I feel very self-satisfied. With Carrie's help, the PowerPoint presentation is complete, data sheets and equipment brochures packaged for shipment with everything else deemed necessary for Vancouver. The technical support team has been formed and necessary departure times identified. The condo is neat and tidy. Windows sparkle, and boxes and crates that had sat untouched for two years have been unpacked, their contents put away or trashed. The cleaning lady had to stop and check to see if she had entered the correct unit upon her arrival that morning. It was the first time she'd been able to vacuum without dodging around boxes and crates.

That morning, I feel great. That ton of weight that I'd carried for the past two years had finally lifted from my shoulders and been put to rest. I had met with Pam. I had to smile, thinking about it. Charley had been right as rain. Pam had needed money. She had tired of life among the trees, left the forest ranger with the Smokey the Bear hat, and was headed for Utah. I had seen a side of her that I had never seen before. She had driven down from Stockton with all her stuff in an old pickup truck with a beat-up camper shell stuck loosely on the truck bed. She had stopped at her sister's place in Van Nuys and was now headed for someplace in Utah named Sugarville. We had lunch at Ruby's on the Pier and then walked along the bike path above the beach. I had realized immediately that it was really all over and was surprised that I was actually relieved. I had written her a check, which she insisted would only be a loan. As I signed my name on the check, I knew it would never be paid back. Hell, it was a final payment on the past. I can't help grinning as I picture her driving that pickup across the desert east of Barstow with the temperature at 110 degrees. I can't help but think she must have been a Mormon pioneer in a previous life.

Sunday evening, while watching the news and flipping through the channels, I'd stopped on a Travel Channel program featuring two men catching salmon from the stern of a charter boat. The location was north of Seattle on Puget Sound. I'd gotten to thinking, *I like to fish, but the only fishing I've done was catching small sand dabs off the local pier.* Now, salmon—that's real fishing. Lying in bed later that evening, I'd still been thinking about those two guys pulling in big salmon. "Damn, I'm going to be in that area anyway. I think I'll go fishing— first class." With that thought in mind, I'd rolled over and fallen asleep.

Monday morning, with Carrie's help, I charter a sportfishing boat out of Seattle for some fishing in the straits of Juan Defuca. For the first time in a long time, I was really getting excited about something. Thanks to Charley, CalMac is footing the bill. My itinerary includes no flying. I intend to drive, make an easy trip north, stopping along the way as the mood dictates, go fishing, then to Vancouver and prepare for the presentation. Once that's over, I'd take the ferry to Seattle and make a leisurely drive home—maybe even stop for some fun and games along the way back. Maybe an ex-girl-friend now living in San Jose is still single. If I could find her phone number, I'd give her a call.

The next morning, I'm ready to hit the road—the car fueled, serviced, and packed with stuff. A lot of the items are things I usually don't pack for a trip and then find later I wished I had; but this time, not having to lug it through an airport, I'm taking all of it.

It's a typical sunny Southern California morning as I pull out on Pacific Coast Highway. The breeze is keeping the palm fronds busy and the smog back against the mountains to the north. Once northbound on the San Diego freeway, Interstate 5 is open highway to Seattle—anyway, that was what I had been told by the young lady at the Auto Club. "Plan on twenty-four hours or so of driving time," she had told me. Moving easily through traffic, I look forward to the trip. In fact, I feel kind of excited. I'm doing something different. In the two years I had owned the car, I had never really driven it any great distance—a trip to Vegas once on a holiday weekend, but that didn't count. I settle in, adjust the seat belt, and hit the CD player. I have no set timetable except being in Seattle in six days. I figure it to be an easy trip, stopping as the spirit moves me.

A sudden electronic buzzing catches me by surprise. It takes a moment to realize that it's the car phone. Punching the remote car speaker, I immediately recognize Carrie's voice. "Hi, Carrie. What's up? I'm just north of Long Beach. Did I forget something?"

"No, no, nothing like that. It's the charter boat service. They called here trying to reach you. The young lady wants to know if you can possibly arrive sooner than planned. There's a large weather front expected to move into the Seattle area in the next few days, and if you could arrive ahead of schedule, they could be well north of the area and miss it. What do you want me to tell them?"

Remembering what the gal at the Auto Club had said, I reply, "Call them back, Carrie. Tell them I should be there sometime late tomorrow afternoon. I'll drive straight through."

"Okay, I'll call. But please, Wesley, don't take any foolish chances. You be careful."

I smile to myself. "I'll be fine, Carrie. I'll send you a salmon from Seattle. Bye-bye." *Well, so much for the easy drive north*, I think to myself. Then, looking at the thermos of coffee sitting next to a bag of donuts, I'm hoping that will hold me until I make a pit stop. The car has always seemed large enough before, for a two-seater; but with all the stuff I've brought along, my six-foot, two-inch frame seems stuffed into the remaining space. Once north of Los Angeles, traffic thins out, and I'm able to maintain a steady seventy-five miles an hour, keeping pace with a string of semitrucks. I had been told that they would make all the speed they could before hitting the Grapevine—the steep grade over Tejon Pass. Once on top, it's all downhill to Bakersfield. Mentally calculating, I figure if I can maintain this pace, I should be able to hit Grants Pass, Oregon, by midnight; but right now, my main target is Bakersfield. The coffee is starting to affect my kidneys, and I really need to walk a bit and stretch my legs in the worst say.

The next segment of the drive from Bakersfield hasn't been too bad, but the drive from Grants Pass to Portland has been the pits. Having been on the road for nearly twenty hours, I'm ready to call it quits. "Crap, I should have flown. I don't know what I was thinking about." Early morning traffic seems heavy with many trucks on the road. Spotting a billboard advertising gas and a restaurant two miles ahead, I move to the right, watching for the off-ramp. Pulling into the parking area, I kill the engine and, for the next few moments, rest my head on the steering wheel. Even the car seems to settle down, needing a rest.

I can hear the engine and exhaust click and creak from the cool morning air. Grabbing my shaving kit from the back seat, I lock the car and head for the restaurant and the men's room. An hour or so later, cleaned up and finished with breakfast, I feel halfway human again and figure I might as well gas up and hit the road for Seattle. It can't be more than two or three more hours, and I can sleep on the boat when I get there. As I approach Seattle from the south, a few raindrops hit the windshield and traffic starts to slow. Unhooking the seat belt, I stretch my cramped legs and shift in the seat.

Stiff, sore, tired, and still mumbling about the decision to drive rather than fly, I prepare to stop, as the traffic lanes ahead are filled with red brake lights. Probably a traffic accident, and I'll bet the rain is the front edge of the weather front the boat people are concerned about. Making a quick decision, I swing to the right, out of the freeway lanes, and onto an exit ramp. There have to be other roads to Seattle, if only I can find one. The paved road winds down to the valley below, and at the bottom, I turn northwest on what seems like a secondary highway. *This doesn't look too bad, and it's headed in the right direction*, I think to myself. *Maybe I'll luck out.*

As I drive, I think back over the past twenty-some hours. Just the thought of a return trip home makes me groan. *If only I had flown . . .* The heavy lurch of the vehicle jars me wide awake. I instantly realize I have fallen asleep at the wheel and the car is leaving the road. As the jolt throws me forward, my last thought before everything goes black is that I haven't refastened my seat belt.

5

CHALLENGE

Life should be like chili: Some
spice, but not too much.
—Julia Child, 1912–2004

The sound of rain on the roof of the car and a tapping noise brought me out of the darkness and back to consciousness. As I shook my head and rubbed a lump on my forehead, my vision started to clear, and I could see that I had ended up in a ditch. Hearing a voice, I turned my head slowly—really slowly—and saw a man tapping on the side window. "Hey there, are you okay? Can you hear me in there? Are you hurt? You okay?"

I nodded, unlocking the car door and haltingly managing to step out of the car. "I, uh, dozed off, I think." Feeling the lump on my forehead, I could tell that it was bleeding.

"Come with me, young fella. Come on over to the house, and Jenny and I will get you fixed up. Then we'll see about getting you out of that ditch." With the old man assisting, I crossed the edge of the field to a small farmhouse. Entering the kitchen, I could immediately feel the warmth generated by an old woodburning stove, and it suddenly dawned on me that it was really cold outside.

Speaking to an elderly woman standing by the doorway watching us enter, the farmer nodded toward me and said, "Jen, this young fella just had a little accident. Help him with that cut while

I get some bandages." Sitting at the kitchen table while holding a wet towel to my head, I relaxed. The aroma of wood burning in the stove blending with the warmth of the room helped lessen the fatigue wracking my body. Man, why didn't I just stay home and let Charley handle this deal? If I had, I could have taken time off and, who knows, maybe put a move on Charley's secretary? Oh yeah—now, here I sat in an old farmhouse bleeding in some lady's dish towel while my car sat stuck in a ditch. This was really one hell of an idea.

My lamenting was interrupted as the farmer returned. "Here, let me put a patch on that cut." Taking the towel, he tilted my head and applied a small bandage. "Shoot, that ain't much of a cut, but that bump will be around for a while. Now, let's see about getting that car of yours back on the road. What kind of a machine is that, anyway? That's the fanciest auto I've ever seen. Sure ain't no Ford. That's for sure. Now y'all sit tight, and I'll go get my tractor. We'll get you going in no time." The woman had left the room, and for the first time, I started to look around.

There was a calendar on the wall. It had a picture of a wild duck in flight and the day/date page below it was for the month of December 1941. A newspaper lay folded on another kitchen chair, and the headline, in big block letters, caught my eye: "US-Japan Dispute over War Materials." The newspaper was dated Friday, December 5. Time started to run through my head. There were some things that don't add up around here. Something's really weird. I must have really smacked my head.

Not knowing what to do, I figured I'd better go out to my car. Leaving the warm house and walking to the car across the field, the cold air cut right through my clothes. Man, it was cold enough to snow. Grabbing my jacket from the car, I made a quick check for damage just as the farmer chugged up in an old Fordson tractor. Using a big manila towrope, the Benz was back on the road in no time. Refusing an offer of payment for his help, the farmer smiled and shook my hand, saying, "Nah, but thanks anyhow. You can just consider it an early Christmas present."

As I started the engine, the old man ducked down and said through the open window, "Just follow the road, and you'll hit the south end of Seattle. Now, you be careful and get some sleep. Good luck to ya, son." As I started to pull away, a 1936 Chevrolet passed me on the left. Both the driver and the passenger stared hard at me and the Benz. As the Benz gathered speed, I could feel that the steering was stiff and the car pulled hard to the left. Damn, something was bent or busted. Maybe I could limp into Seattle, where I could find a dealer.

Reaching over and hitting the Seek button on the radio, I got nothing but static. Punching the AM button, I was really startled to hear Christmas music. Changing stations, I listened, totally confused, as the commentator talked about the upcoming Rose Bowl Parade and the Rose Bowl football game to be played in Pasadena on New Year's Day 1942. Well, if this is really early December of 1941, that guy wouldn't know a war is going to force the Rose Bowl game to be played in Durham, North Carolina. Remembering the data from my Sports Trivia games, without thinking, I said to myself, "January second, Oregon State over Duke, 20–16."

Trying to focus on the road while attempting to make sense out of all that had happened was mindboggling. This was crazy. If this was happening, the only explanation was a time warp, and those things only happened in movies. More confused than ever, body hurting and head aching and the car becoming more difficult to steer, I pulled to the side of the road, letting a couple more old cars pass me; and as before, drivers and passengers stared at me and the car.

Taking a couple of aspirin from my shaving kit, I washed them down with a shot of cold coffee from my thermos. Damn—old cars, old newspapers, and Christmas music in May. I'd figure out what's going on later. Right now, first things first. Pulling back onto the road, I spotted a mailbox just a short distance ahead. Hanging below the box was a sign: For Sale. Adjacent to the post was an overgrown gravel driveway. Hoping I might find a telephone, I pulled into the driveway. At the top of the driveway sat a small house, half hidden by dormant fruit trees. As I stopped adjacent to the old house, it was readily apparent that the placed was empty and had been for a long time.

Farther back and to the far side of the house stood an old garage covered with dead blackberry bushes and doors hanging agape. Farther back still stood a water storage tank and a small shed with a tattered electrical line running to it from the house, which I guessed would be the pump house. Well, that caps it. I quit. I'll figure it all out later. With that thought in mind, I drove the car into the old garage and killed the engine. Pulling my coat up tight and tilting the seat back all the way, I dropped off into a deep and badly needed sleep. As the growing darkness pushed its way into the old garage, the coldness nudged me awake. Groaning, I brought the seat to an upright position, trying to remember all the pieces of the puzzle that put me there.

Starting the engine, I turned the heat on high and again started to search for a local radio station. Fifteen minutes of listening to various stations, I was again totally confused. If I believed what I'd seen and heard, it was Friday, December 5, 1941—at least, it was where I was then. Killing the engine and getting out of the car, I stretched to work out all the kinks and stiffness. I could see the back porch of the old house a short distance away. All the windows I could see in back were boarded over. Stopping to take a leak against the garage door, I thought to myself, *Maybe I ought to write my name, just for kicks, and stake out a claim.*

Hunched over because of the cold dampness, I headed for the porch and approached the back door. Trying the doorknob, I was totally unprepared to feel it turn and find the door unlocked. Giving the door a push, I entered an empty room that, even in the semi-darkness, I could tell had been the kitchen. Old linoleum nailed in various places around the edges covered the floor. A rusty old cast-iron woodstove piped to a hot water tank behind it stood next to a water-stained sink. Moving toward the front of the house, I passed a bathroom on the left of a short hallway and a room on the right that had most likely been a bedroom. The end of the hallway opened into a large room with rectangular windows facing the highway at the bottom of the drive. A cold breeze could be felt coming down the chimney of the small fireplace built into the wall.

A straight-backed wooden chair, paint chipped and peeling, stood like a lone sentinel in the empty room. Looking out between the boards nailed haphazardly over one window, I could see the lights of what appeared to be a small diner and a Texaco gas station at a crossroad intersection about a quarter mile away. Returning to the car, I couldn't help but try the radio one more time; but as before, all programming was geared to the upcoming holiday—Christmas. Dammit, this couldn't be real. Things like this didn't really happen. I couldn't believe what's going on.

Turning off the radio, I rubbed the lump on my forehead. Yeah, that pain was real enough. Okay, I was going to have to play the game. I'd take it one step at a time. I couldn't drive anywhere without attracting attention. I couldn't tell this story without looking like some kind of a loony. I was cold and hungry and thought I'd better stay out of sight until I could figure out what was going on and put together a good game plan. Getting out of the car, I went to the trunk and removed the small overnight bag, grabbed my pair of leather boots thrown in at the last moment before leaving home and a small yellow cardboard box sealed in plastic wrap. Carrying everything into the house, I placed all of it on the floor near the old stove. Knowing dry, unpainted wood burned with little smoke, I systematically started to break up the old wooden chair taken from the front room of the house for firewood. Next on the list was the small yellow cardboard box—a compact emergency kit. Like so many other Southern Californians, after the last earthquake, I had purchased several of those small kits—one I kept in my condo and one in the car. Each kit contained food bars, a sealed container of water, a thermal blanket, and other miscellaneous items designed to support one person for three days.

Using matches from the kit, a small fire began to take the chill from the immediate area of the kitchen. As I left the firebox door on the stove open, a soft glow of light filtered through the room. Munching an energy bar, I started to unpack my small overnight case, laying everything out on the thermal blanket. An hour later, dressed in chinos, a Pendleton shirt over a turtleneck sweater, and my hiking boots, I felt that this Southern Californian sun-loving boy was ready to face the crappy Pacific Northwest weather outside. Walking to the front of the house and checking the highway below, I could see that the traffic was light. The lousy weather was keeping most people at home. Right now I needed real food and hot coffee.

Checking to ensure that the fire had pretty well burned down, leaving only glowing coals, I grabbed my shaving kit and, donning my leather jacket, walked out the back door. Bad weather or not, the little diner down the road drew like a magnet. However, a sink full of hot water and a flush toilet were high on the priority list also. As I approached the diner, I could see several locals at the small counter. Entering, the aroma of food and fresh coffee was like a physical blow to my body. Walking past the others who were deep in conversation, I passed a little Christmas tree and the jukebox near the end of the counter and took the end stool.

Without asking, the counterman placed a steaming hot cup of coffee and a menu in front of me. The coffee was almost too hot to drink, but it was the nectar of the gods. Looking at the menu, I could not help but grin: the price for a steak dinner was less than what a small popcorn and a Coke had cost me at the last movie I had gone to. Ordering a steak, two eggs, hash browns, and a piece of apple pie, I headed for the restroom at the rear of the diner for a welcome visit.

Returning to the counter, my food was waiting with a fresh cup of coffee. As I ate, I couldn't help hearing the conversation at the other end of the counter. Glancing to my left, I could see a sailor in uniform, a gas station attendant (probably from the station next door), and the counterman conversing over a newspaper lying open on the counter in front of them. "I'm telling you, guys," the sailor was saying, "look what's going on. The Germans are kicking hell out of the English and beating up the French real quick. And all the while, the Japs are running roughshod through China. Here we sit, giving all that lend- lease war material to the English so they can continue to wage war, but we stopped selling oil and scrap metal to Japan. Now, does that sound like being neutral? I'm not siding with the Japs, but face it: they're not going to sit still and put up with that crap."

The station attendant sat his coffee cup down, pointed his finger at the sailor, and answered, "Come on, Dick. You know what Congress said: the US won't get involved in any foreign wars. Come on, pal, you military guys are just itching to shoot all those big guns at somebody."

The sailor shook his head and replied hotly, "Oh yeah? Well, I'll tell you this, Vernon: I might be an eighteen-year-old boot seaman, but I really believe we're going to get pulled into this mess regardless of what you think." The young sailor paused and pulled a pack of Luckys out of his peacoat pocket, lit one, and blew smoke at the ceiling. "All the scuttlebutt around the base as well as guys on the ships in port think the fuse has already been lit."

The counterman, having noticed that I was listening to the verbal exchange, pointed at the newspaper and asked, "What do you think, my friend? What's your opinion? Vern here doesn't think we'll get pulled into a shooting war, and Dick here," pointing at the sailor, "thinks the Japs are being pushed into a position that they will have to pull the trigger."

The last thing I wanted was to get involved. I smiled and replied, "Well, I just don't know what to think anymore."

The sailor, sensing my hesitation, looked around and said, "You civilians had better get ready because sure as hell we're going to be in it neck-deep. I'm willing to bet money on it right now!"

Having finished my pie and third cup of coffee, I stood up, placed some bills on the counter, and walked toward the door. Opening it, I turned to the three men and said, "Probably by this time next week, we will all have a different view of things. That was a great meal. Thanks."

Walking back, I went directly to the shed and opened the trunk of the Benz. Unloading the remainder of my luggage and grabbing the portable AM/FM radio cassette, I returned to the kitchen. As I stoked the few embers still glowing with the remaining wood, the small flames provided some welcome heat. As I left the fire grate door open, the small fire provided enough light to allow sorting out the items I thought would be needed. My decision was to relocate to Seattle, take on a new identity, and get lost in the crowd: a new life. Who knows, maybe later getting back to Southern California, buying up some orange groves, and getting ready for the postwar building boom? Maybe even invest in some Xerox, IBM, and Revlon stock. As long as I know what's in the future, I might as well use it to my advantage.

The car would have to be left behind. Maybe I could get it later, but right now it would attract too much attention. That, I did not need. Working quickly, I packed all the extra stuff I wouldn't take with me into the trunk of the Benz and locked it up. Back in the kitchen, I checked out my wallet: credit cards would be worthless. I'd have to get along with the cash I had with me—about $600. But hey, that's a small fortune in 1941 dollars. That should hold me over until I got settled.

Saturday
December 6, 1941

Bright and early, I was up and about. The floor was hard, and I could see my breath in the air. Water out of the hot tap was a little rusty but lukewarm. The small fire in the kitchen stove warmed the water, heating coils enough to take the chill off, but shaving and showering was invigorating, to say the least. Needing a wake-up fix of black coffee, I bundled up, closed the house, and headed down the road to the diner.

That morning, more traffic was on the highway, and I could see that business at the diner was booming. Enjoy it, people, because tomorrow the world goes to hell in a handbasket. As I approached the diner, my love of old cars brought an unanticipated smile to my face. Parked next to the door was a 1937 Packard 120 four-door sedan. I wondered if the owner would trade for a 1992 Mercedes Benz with a busted-up front wheel. Upon entering, much to my surprise, I saw the sailor from the night before.

I took the counter stool next to him and nodded. "Good morning. How's it going?" During the next hour or so and many cups of coffee, we sat then talked and became acquainted. Being a friendly guy, he liked to talk. I pumped him for all the information I could. In this manner, I learned his name and a little about him personally. His name was Richard L. Dickson, nicknamed Dick. He had lied about his age and joined the Naval Reserve about a year ago and was then stationed at Sand Point Naval Air Station, just north of downtown Seattle. The counterman was his brother-in-law, Donald, married to Dick's sister, Marie. He told me how the whole valley southeast of them belonged to Japanese truck farmers. Of particular note, the old house where I was currently camped out unbeknownst to others belonged to Vernon, who owned and operated the Texaco gas station next to the diner. I told him I was from Southern California and had come north looking for work, explaining that I was skilled in the use of metal-turning and machine-shop equipment. Not wanting to delve too deeply into my present situation, I outlined my plan to find a place to stay in Seattle and find a job. "There have to be shipyards and aircraft plants that could use my skills. What's the best way into Seattle?"

Dick replied, "My seventy-two-hour liberty is up tomorrow, and I have to be back at Sand Point before midnight. If you want a ride, I'd be glad to give you a lift. I know of a couple of boarding houses that can't be too expensive. You can get settled in and start looking for a job on Monday. How does that sound?" Agreeing to meet at the diner the next afternoon, Dick left to go see his girlfriend, who lived nearby.

After he left, I finished my coffee and thought, *I might as well go over and talk to Vern about the old house.* Finding him fixing a flat tire, I introduced myself and said, "I understand you own that old house down the road that's for sale."

Vern placed the tire iron on the workbench and said, "Yeah, it was my dad's place. He passed on a year ago, and it's been sitting empty ever since. You want to buy it?"

"No, but I'd like to rent it for a while. I want to store some stuff in the big shed out back."

"Well, I guess we can work something out. What's it worth to you?"

I grinned and said, "How about twenty-five dollars a month and I'll give you the first and last month payment up front."

Startled, Vern stuck his hand out and said, "Mr. Jenner, that's a deal. Hell, for that, you can use the house too, if you want."

Having signed a rental agreement and returned to the house, I checked the garage and ensured that the car trunk was locked and the car alarm activated. Securing the garage doors with a lock Vern had provided, I felt pretty good about things. I might be able to salvage everything after all. Now, the waiting game began.

6

DAY OF INFAMY

Where in hell is Oahu?
—Anonymous, 1941

Early afternoon
December 7, 1941

I'd been pacing the floor all morning, wondering when this quiet day was going to come apart at the seams. I'd decided to stay out of sight until the time to meet Dick. Knowing that a west Seattle bus stopped at the intersection by the diner at 4:00 p.m., my backup plan B was to be on that bus if everything else goes to hell. Earlier, having found enough wood outside, I had built a fire in the fireplace, and the house was warming up. That, plus the morning fire in the kitchen stove, had provided enough hot water for a good shower and shave. Water was still a little rusty but better than using the kitchen sink.

Looking at my Rolex, it was just a few minutes past 1:00 p.m. on the West Coast. In Hawaii, I knew that the Japanese were in the process of shattering the American fleet in Pearl Harbor. I'd read about this in history books and seen it on television, but now I was going to experience it firsthand. Reaching over to the open suitcase, I flicked on the portable radio. The announcer, in a highly excited voice, was telling all his listeners, "We bring you more important information concerning the sneak attack on US military installations on the Hawaiian island of Oahu. Authorities have not announced the scope of damage, but this station has learned from private sources on-site that the raid hit the island about eight o'clock Hawaiian time and has continued for several hours. The naval base at Pearl Harbor is shrouded with smoke, and extensive damage can be seen. The city of Honolulu has received some damage, but the major thrust has been at the military bases of Hickam Field, Schofield Barracks, Wheeler Field, and naval facilities at Pearl Harbor. American sea and air patrols are searching for the Japanese fleet from which the attack was launched. We have received official information that all military personnel are to return to their assigned duty stations. A state of war exists. All law enforcement personnel are to report to their offices and await further direction. Again, this is an official broadcast. Stay tuned to this station for further updates and directions as they are made available."

As the announcement ended, the national anthem filled the airways. I thought I'd better check the car one more time and saddle up to make a move when the timing was right. Stepping out off the back porch, I heard sirens as several police cars roared by on the road below the house. Well, old Dick hit the nail right on the head. He was probably well on his way to Sand Point by now. It looked like I had better plan on the bus. I decided I'd best be on that sucker at 4:00 p.m.

Having checked the Benz and rechecking the gear piled by the back door, I made one more walk through the house. Other than the old chair I had busted up for firewood, I hadn't been a bad tenant. It was hard to believe it had only been three days since the world turned backward. I only wished I could return to my own time. I'd enjoyed just about all I could stand. It was three fifteen, so let the show begin.

Bundled up against the weather with my stuff in a duffel bag, I headed down the road toward the diner and whatever the future had in store.

As I approached the diner, several automobiles were readily visible parked haphazardly by the door. Skipping the diner, where there were people, I headed straight for the gas station. Vern was nowhere in sight, and a stranger was standing in the doorway. Setting my bags by the gas pumps, I asked the man standing there, "Where's Vern? I wanted to see him. There's a bus at four, and I'd like to see him before I leave."

The man nodded and answered, "He's over at the diner. I'll go get him. Why don't you wait inside? It's kind of cold out there." With that, he buttoned his jacket and went out the door. Stepping into the counter area, which was filled with cans of oil, fan belts, and other automotive items, I waited while thinking I'd really like a cup of coffee but I'd better just hang tight. With that thought, I remembered the energy bar in my jacket pocket—the last one from the emergency kit. As I started to unwrap it, two men stepped into the small space. As I turned, I saw that both men held pistols pointed at me. In a very firm voice, the man nearest me said, "Put your hands in the air and turn around. Do it now!" Startled, I raised my hands—the partially unwrapped bar still in my right hand.

"Wait a minute. Hold it. Easy. Don't shoot. I haven't done anything. I'm just waiting for the bus to Seattle."

Motioning with the gun, one of the men said, "Turn around and be quiet. There isn't going to be a bus ride for you. Turn around!" As I turned, the second man pulled my arms down behind my back, handcuffed me, and then patted me down, looking for any weapons I might have hidden on me. The SOB made me drop my energy bar. "Okay, now, nice and slow, walk outside." The second man had stepped ahead and waited by the open door of the diner. He still held a gun in his hand, and I could see it was a .45-caliber model 1911, a service automatic, and I realized this guy was something more than a local cop, maybe a federal guy, but what for? The second man was the one in control, and his manners and tone of voice left no doubt. Pointing at the closest booth with his gunhand, he said, "Sit down." I did as I was told. Standing some distance away by the counter were Seaman Dickson, Vern, and Donald, the owner of the diner. The man in control looked at the three of them and asked, "Is this the guy?" No one said anything, just nodded in the affirmative.

"What the hell is going on here, anyway? Who are you guys, and why am I in cuffs?" I asked.

"Just take it easy. I'll ask the questions. You answer them," replied the second man. Sitting down on the opposite side of the booth, he turned to Donald and asked, "How about a cup of coffee. This has been one hell of a day." Then, looking at me, he said, "I'm James Corrigan. I'm the FBI bureau chief in this area. The big question is, who the hell are you, and what are you doing here? It's been reported that you've been asking a lot of questions about naval bases, defense plants, and other big industries."

Beginning to feel my anger rise, I looked around and stopped to stare at Corrigan. "Look, I'm an American citizen, and you can't do this to me without just cause."

Corrigan stared right back and replied, "This country is in war status, and you've been identified as being a suspicious person."

Shaking my head, I said, "Hey, come on. I'm new to this area, and I'm looking for work. You can't arrest me for that."

Corrigan took a drink of coffee, lit a cigarette, smiled, and replied, "Right now, in the name of national defense, I can do damned near anything I want. Until I'm sure you're not involved in some kind of espionage, you're being held for passing counterfeit money." Pointing at the diner's owner, Corrigan said, "This man tells me you have been in his establishment several times to eat in the last couple of days. Each time you paid him with excellent fakes—correct paper and ink, but whoever printed them really goofed up: wrong series numbers, wrong dates, and the current secretary of the treasury signs his name Henry Morgenthau Jr., and that isn't who signed the bills you've been passing." Even in all the confusion, I did notice that Vern hadn't offered up the bills that I had given him as rent payment. Way to go, Vern!

Concurrent with the questioning, the other two agents had retrieved my duffel bags and were searching through them. "Hey, Jim, you'd better come over here and take a look at what we're finding in this guy's bag." Lying on the counter was my 35 mm Nikon camera, a compact set of field binoculars, and my portable AM/FM radio / cassette player. "This is real high-tech stuff, and it's all made in Japan." With that comment, my body went limp, and I suddenly felt sick, with one thought in mind: *Man, they're going to shoot me sure as hell.*

Corrigan slipped out of the booth and stood. "Okay, guys, gather it all up and load it into a car. We're going to the naval base and taking this dude with us." Turning to Dickson, he said, "You come with us. I'll let your commanding officer know where you'll be." The other agents headed for the door with me in tow and piled into their cars.

Turning, Corrigan gave his attention to the other two men still standing by the counter, looking dumbfounded. Pointing his finger directly at them, he gave them a warning that curled their toes. "What you have just seen and all that you have witnessed is a highly confidential matter and is not to be discussed or revealed to anyone. Do you understand? Not to anyone. If either of you says one word concerning what has just happened, I'll see to it that you are charged with conduct detrimental to the war effort and sent to a federal prison. Is that understood?"

"Yes, sir," both men answered in unison as Corrigan turned to leave. As the door of the diner clicked shut, Vern turned and ran for the men's room. Corrigan climbed into the closest sedan and checked that I was in the back seat under guard. He directed the driver to head for Sand Point and signaled the other cars to follow.

Knowing that he should check his prisoner into the downtown federal facility, Corrigan felt there was more to this matter than met the eye and felt the security of the US Marine Corps at Sand Point was more to his liking. The drive to Seattle was slow, as we were stopped at many hastily erected checkpoints. Buildings were dark, and traffic was sparse. As we drove in silence, I wondered what else was among my possessions that might get me into deeper trouble. Then, like a flash, it hit me like a bolt of lightning: My god, every cent I have with me is worthless and will be considered fake, just like the bills. Oh, Lord, let this be a dream. Please, Lord, let me wake up from this nightmare.

As the cars approached the naval station main gate, well-armed sentries stopped the caravan. Corrigan got out and entered the guardhouse. I watched him as he talked on the phone. Within minutes, a military vehicle pulled to the gate and stopped. Corrigan got in and waved the others to follow. About two hours later, they had taken my watch. I was in a guarded cellblock dressed in blue coveralls. All my clothes and baggage had been taken away shortly after we'd arrived. Completely stressed out, I curled up on the cell bunk and pulled the single blanket up to my chin. Lying in the bunk, wondering what would happen next, I watched a spider spinning a web from the caged light fixture high overhead. I thought, *I guess that's the situation I'm in. One big web, and I'm caught right in the middle of it.*

From down the hall, I heard people approaching. Corrigan, with two armed guards, stopped at my cell, and one tough-looking Marine unlocked the cell door. "On your feet, Jenner. Come with me," Corrigan growled as he started down the corridor. I followed, flanked by the two Marines. After a walk through a maze of hallways, we entered a brightly lit conference room. The same men who had been with Corrigan at the diner surrounded a table in the center of the room. On it was everything I had been wearing as well as everything I had packed lying there. Sitting off to one side, a young woman was watching us as we entered the room. Corrigan motioned for me to a chair set apart from the others.

"Okay, Mr. Jenner, let's talk. Over there on the table, we have everything you were carrying with you or were wearing. We have gone through your clothing and all of your belongings, including your wallet. It seems that you must be quite a worldwide traveler. Your boots are from Italy, French jeans, Korean shirts, and most conspicuous, highly technical equipment all made by the Japanese. Your wallet contained more of the currency you tried to use previously and other documents, all dated 50 years or more in the future. But let's start here." Turning to the table, he picked up a small object, turned, and held it up so all present could see it. "This, Mr. Jenner, is a Japanese ten-yen coin found in the corner seam of your duffel bag."

I couldn't catch my breath. Man, that was like a sucker punch—really catching me off guard. My habit of throwing small change in my luggage case instead of carrying it in my pocket was digging the hole even deeper. "Any comments, Mr. Jenner?"

"Well, yes, dammit, I have." It had been a long, trying day for me also, so I figured I'd better establish my territory. Speaking directly to Corrigan, I said, "I would like a cup of hot coffee, and I will probably need a couple of refills." Smiling at the young lady, I then looked again directly at Jim Corrigan. "You'd better sit down. This will be a long story." Corrigan nodded to one of his agents, who then walked over to a typical Navy coffee mess in the far corner of the room and drew two mugs of coffee, placing one where Corrigan had taken a seat and the other on the far corner of the table where I was seated. One sip of that hot coffee confirmed something I had learned from visiting many military facilities incidental to my work: The US Navy makes the best cup of coffee in the world, bar none. Nectar of the gods.

Again glancing in the direction of the young lady, I started a story that I knew no one would believe. "On Thursday, May 12, 1994, I left Huntington Beach, California, to drive to Seattle, Washington, for a combined business/vacation trip . . ."

Hours later, after a myriad of questions and answers, I was dead tired, my head ached, my back was stiff, and I was in desperate need of a men's room. Corrigan stood, saying, "That's a great story. You ought to put it on paper and sell it as a science fiction novel."

Pushed to the point that I just didn't give a damn anymore, I retorted, "You people need a window in your navel to see where you're going. You think I'm making all this up? I'll tell you a little history from my 1994 history book: In a couple of days, the British will lose two major warships to Japanese dive bombers in Malaya, and the next day, December 11, 1941, both Germany and Italy will declare war on the US. How's that for science fiction, Mr. Bureau Chief? Now, in what direction is the men's room?"

Corrigan shook his head and motioned to one of the Marines. "Take him to the head and then bring him back here. Remember, what you have witnessed is not to be discussed. Understand?"

The Marine saluted. "Yes, sir." And he escorted me down the hall. Thank God, I'd begun to think I wouldn't make it in time.

Meanwhile, back in the conference room, Corrigan waved at the other agent who was leaning back in his chair. "Okay, O'Brien, wake up and quit yawning. Get that Jenner guy a warm jacket. We are going to go out to that farmhouse he was talking about and check it out. I don't give a damn what time it is. We'd better check it out and investigate everything we can, PDQ. Get some big flashlights and meet us at the front gate." Turning to the girl, he said, "Susan, I'm sorry, kid, but you will have to take all of your notes and get back to the office and, using every priority you have to, get all the info you can on this guy Jenner. Get the Los Angeles office to find anything they can. We'll meet back here at . . ." Looking at his watch, he was shocked to see it was already 12:40 a.m. "We'll meet at 1300 hours. That gives you about twelve hours to get all you can. Also, pass on to the home office what he said about Germany and Italy on the eleventh. I think it's all horse manure."

A short time later, Corrigan and two bureau agents, with me in tow, were at the main gate of the base, sitting in a military sedan. Additionally, a four-by-four truck with a small contingent of armed Marines under the command of the sergeant of the guard was also waiting to roll. The ride back out to the farmhouse was long and uncomfortable. The back seat of a 1940 Plymouth sedan was tight, and I couldn't stretch my legs enough to keep them from cramping. Finally passing the diner, now dark and empty, I knew we were almost there. With lights out, both car and four-by-four stopped on the edge of the road short of the driveway leading up to the house. In the cold, predawn darkness, Corrigan quietly gave directions to the group gathered around him. Grabbing my arm, he told me, "You stay close to me. Any false move will be the last one you make. Believe me, okay?" I nodded but said nothing. "Sergeant, deploy your men around the building. Don't let anyone slip away. I don't know what to expect, so be alert."

As we approached the old house, Corrigan directed the sergeant to deploy his people. "I'll give you five minutes to be in position.

Then I'm going in. Remember, we'll be inside that building, and I don't want any of my people shot."

"Yes, sir," the Marine replied. "But, sir, it's still pretty dark. How about waiting for first light?"

Corrigan, shaking his head, said, "No, we go now. Move your people out." Approaching the back of the house, Corrigan waited a moment and then grabbed the back of my jacket and pushed me forward. "Okay, wise guy, anyone in there shoots, you get it first." As I pushed the door open and entered through the kitchen, a quick search revealed the house is empty. I wanted to say, "Ha, I told you so!" But common sense told me to keep my mouth shut.

As we moved to the back porch, I commented in a respectful voice, "Just like I left it. Even the yellow emergency ration box is right there."

Ignoring me, Corrigan told Agent O'Brien, "Go tell the sergeant that his people can stand easy. They can smoke if they wish but stay alert and don't wander about. Also, bring the vehicles up here."

With his flashlight, Corrigan waved at the agent by the porch and said, "Follow me, Dave. Let's look in the old shed." Pulling me along with him, Corrigan headed for the garage. Trying to hold a straight face, I couldn't help thinking, *This ought to be interesting.* Hell, I was actually starting to enjoy this little scenario. With me again in tow, Corrigan, flashlight in hand, unlocked the garage doors and pulled them open.

"Jeez, boss, will you look at that car? Look at the emblem. It's a German Mercedes." Moving inside the shed on the driver's side of the car, Corrigan shone his flashlight through the driver's side window and reached for the door handle. As he touched the handle, a sharp siren wailed into the night, and the car's headlights started to flash. Startled, Corrigan lunged back from the car and, in doing so, smacked his head on a small storage shelf protruding from the garage wall, falling to his knees. Marines dropped their smokes and crouched, rifles ready, trying to figure out where the siren was coming from.

Corrigan, having regained his feet, backed out of the garage, rubbing his head. I yelled at him, "Push the red button on the key chain!" Doing so, the alarm stopped, and in the dead silence, dogs could be heard barking for miles around. In available light, I could see that everyone was staring at me.

As both vehicles came up the drive, their headlights lit up the area. The agent named Dave, gun in hand, yelled to Corrigan, "What the hell happened? We just woke up every farmer within two miles!"

Ignoring the comment, Corrigan pointed to the military sedan. "Get in. We're going back. Sergeant, keep your people here and don't let any locals get near this place. And shut the shed doors. Come daylight, I'll have a big van out here to load everything up and haul it back to the base under wraps." Motioning me again toward the sedan, he couldn't miss the grin on my face and said in a low voice, "Okay, wise ass, you've had your fun. Get in the car."

It was a quiet ride back to Sand Point. Back in my cell and still fully dressed, I crawled into my bunk and pulled the blanket over my head. For some reason, my last thought before falling asleep was about the young lady in the conference room. She was not only a real looker; she also had great legs.

The noise of the cell door opening jarred me awake. Aw, man, now what? Carrying a tray, the guard said, "Okay, out of the sack. I'm bringing your meal."

Rubbing sleep from my eyes, I mumbled to the guy, "I need sleep, not breakfast."

Laughing, the guard replied, "Wake up, buddy boy. This is dinner. You've slept all day long. When you're finished, I'll escort you to the shower so you can clean up." I picked at my meal.

On the other side of the base, in the commanding officer's conference room, Jim Corrigan and Susan McEuen sat at a large table with a mixed group of military and civilians. The table was covered with green felt typical ward-room decor. Scattered coffee cups and small piles of paper lay intermingled with brass ashtrays that some gunner's mate had made out of five-inch gunpowder casings. Cigarette smoke hung in the air as the group discussed the day's events centered on the congressional adoption of a declaration of war with Japan. All conversation stopped and everyone stood as the base commander entered, accompanied by another high-ranking Navy officer, followed by several aides. The CO waved everyone to their seats. "Thank you for being here today. I apologize for the short notice. Now, before we close for the day, let me turn this meeting over to Captain William Anderson, commander, Northwest Sea Frontier, who wishes to say a few closing words. Captain?"

"Good evening. At the present time, I am responsible for Sea Frontier security in this district. Forget formalities. We've got a lot to do, and I wish to make this short. This afternoon, all district commands and forces afloat have been given newly assigned area responsibilities. We gathered here this afternoon to further outline these areas of concern and determine military and civilian sector guidelines. I thank you for being here today. As you leave, each of you will be given handouts identifying particular areas and assignments. This is classified information and is to be handled accordingly." Stopping to light a cigarette, he blew smoke at the ceiling and continued. "The general population is confused and frightened. We have received unconfirmed reports of signal fires on various beaches to Japanese ships off the coast, acts of sabotage, and secret radio broadcasts. Let me say again, these are unconfirmed. It is the government's intent to find and intern all Japanese foreign nationals. Additionally, action in accordance with Executive Order 9066, yet to be finalized, will be taken to relocate all Japanese civilians inland, away from the Pacific Coast, from Mexico to the Canadian border."

Walking to the end of the table and picking up my 35 mm Nikon camera, he turned and held it in the air. "People, we are fighting an enemy with years of experience in China learning how to wage war. This camera was just taken from a person currently in our custody. It was made in Japan. Is it junk? Well, let me tell you: it is so technically advanced we have nothing to compare it with. That small radio there on the table has shortwave capability and was also made in Japan. It requires no tubes of any sort and is powered by four small dry-cell batteries. What are your thoughts? I'll tell you mine: It scares the hell out of me. We are at war with a powerful nation with unknown capabilities. We are in a world of hurt and have a lot of catching up to do. Can we do it? Yes, we can, but it will take time and we must all do our part."

With that short speech, he sat down. The base commanding officer stood and addressed all present. "There will be follow-up action to be identified later. Until further notice, what you have accomplished, seen, and heard this day is classified top secret and not to be discussed with others not cleared by the war department. Thank you for your combined efforts and all that was accomplished today as well as for being here this evening. This meeting is now ended."

As the attendees filed out, Captain Anderson motioned Jim Corrigan and the base commander to stay. Alone in the room, the three sat at the table. Looking at the items on the table, Captain Anderson asked, "Jim, tell me about this man you are holding here on base. I approve of your decision to bring him here rather than turn him over to the defense department officials. We can always do that later."

Corrigan pulled at his tie and unbuttoned the top button of his shirt. He quickly told them about my capture and what he considered the wild story of my having been transported from the year 1994 back to present day. "We are still in the process of investigating the information we have been able to gather. This is what we have determined as of now."

Having anticipated such a request at some point, Corrigan decided to tell it like it was. "Captain, his given residence in California does not exist. The location is nothing but oil wells and orange groves. There is no record of the name 'Wesley Jenner,' and the business location provided is nonexistent—only a large orange grove. At the time of his arrest, he had in his possession all that you see on the table—all made in Japan or other foreign countries. The automobile he was driving is a Mercedes Benz of German manufacture, so far advanced it's unbelievable. Did you happen to notice the two wristwatches lying on the table? One is a typical, expensive dress Rolex, which he was wearing when apprehended. The other, due to its condition, appears to be a watch worn when at work. Notice the scratches and wear on the band. However, it is extremely accurate, powered by a tiny battery, and it has no moving parts. It shows the time, day, date, and month, and when you press a small button on the side of the case, the damned thing lights up so you can read it in the dark. I'm telling you, Captain, I don't believe in science fiction, but everything this guy has is strictly out of a Buck Rogers comic book."

Lighting a smoke, Corrigan could see that both naval officers were stunned. Captain Anderson shook his head and said, "Okay, okay. Now, listen to me. I've been in this business long enough to not believe everything I hear and only half of what I see. This guy scares the hell out of me, and I believe he is only part of what is something much bigger. I'm glad you got him in custody before he could do any real damage. Let the military technical people look at what you've gathered up. Maybe they can figure out how to apply the knowledge gained to help our side for a change. Corrigan, pump this guy for everything you can get out of him. If, by some unbelievable chance, this guy is from the future, then find out what mistakes we can avoid and what we have to do to win this damned war we find ourselves in."

Turning on his heels, he left the room with his aides in fast pursuit, followed by the base commanding officer. Walking down the hall to where Susan was waiting, Corrigan shrugged his shoulders and told her, "Get hold of the base commander first thing in the morning and tell him we need that sailor, Dickson. If possible, we need him assigned to us. He has at least talked with this guy and isn't a strange face. Between the two of you, get this guy's life history or whatever. Until we get more people, that's your assignment. The rest of the department has their work cut out for them, as you heard at the afternoon meeting. Set up a timeframe when you can brief me daily on your progress. Got it?"

Smiling wanly, Susan nodded and said, "Good night, Mr. Corrigan."

7

THE BYSTANDER

If he can walk, draft him!
—Henry L. Stimson, forty-fifth secretary of war, 1942

Sand Point Naval Air Station
December 10, 1941

I was awake before reveille. Automatically, I looked at my bare wrist. Damn, I really missed my watch. I bet that SOB Corrigan was wearing it. This had to be Tuesday, I think. I was losing track of time. Not used to being cooped up in a small space, I had tossed and turned all night. Shortly after, reveille sounded the duty guard moved several other prisoners out of the cellblock and informed them they were free to return to their places of duty.

"Leave the booze alone and quit fighting in the local bars. Save it for the Japs. If there's a next time, you'll lose stripes and be on restriction. Now, get out of here. There's a real war to fight."

Moving to my cell, he said, "Come on, Jenner. The shower is all yours for the time being, but shake a leg. We have to get to the mess hall. It's going to close earlier from now on—longer duty hours for all personnel."

After eating, I was really surprised when the guard threw me a foul-weather jacket and told me I was going to another building, not back to the cell. It was overcast and cold, and a light rain was falling.

The wind blowing off Lake Washington felt good on my face, and the feeling of wide-open space was like a tonic to the soul. Directed to a small cement building a short distance away, I was ushered into an even smaller office and told to wait.

Through the reinforced glass window, I watched as a large seaplane, a PBY-5 Catalina, was towed out of a hangar and moved down the tarmac. A fuel truck and a small vehicle with an auxiliary generator followed close behind. Looking around, I saw that the room was sparsely furnished with a minimum of old office equipment and had the smell and appearance of having been a storage space until just recently. A desk, four chairs, and a coffee table took up most of the space. Against the wall behind the desk was a credenza holding a hotplate, a coffee percolator, and an assortment of mismatched cups looking totally out of place. The one decor item was a large map of the United States hanging on the wall, only forty-eight states. Looking at the credenza, I wondered if anyone had started a pot of coffee. Just as I was about to check out the coffeepot, the door opened. Much to my pleasant surprise, the young lady from the conference room walked in and shut the door. Moving to the desk, she set down a briefcase and a stack of papers, then turned, and nodded. "Good morning, Mr. Jenner. My name is Susan McEuen, and just so you know, there is an armed guard outside the door."

Taking a seat at the desk, she motioned me to a chair facing her. "I am an administrative specialist with the Department of the Navy. This is the situation: Officially, you are being held for investigation of passing counterfeit money. However, you know as well as I that you are also under investigation for espionage during time of war. You are an unknown and have no identification or official residence that can be confirmed. You have given an explanation of your purpose for being in the Seattle area, which is, quite frankly, unbelievable. For reasons of national defense, you are being detained on a military base under guard. Now, if you wish to cooperate, we can get down to business. If not, then I'm out of here, and they will throw your fanny in a federal prison and shoot you as a spy. Got the picture?" I couldn't help but admire this beautiful young woman—her stature, her poise, her whatever; but damn, if she played sports, she might be a cheerleader but with the disposition of a badass linebacker.

Looking directly at her as I formulated my reply, I couldn't help but notice her dark-green eyes matched the color of her jacket and her shiny bronze hair gave her a startling resemblance to the movie actress Susan Hayward. "Well, Ms. McEuen—it is *miss*, isn't it? Seeing how you put it that way, I'll go with option one. Where do you want to start?"

For the next three and a half hours, I related my life story from being born in Huntington Beach, schooling, college, failed marriage, my work, business trips—everything right up until the time I drove into the ditch. While taking a break, Susan called Corrigan's office to get someone to drive out and verify the "car in the ditch" story. During the course of the morning discussions, without either one of us being aware, formality had faded, and we had both come to address each other by our first names.

After lunch, Susan decided to try another avenue of questioning. Now sitting directly across each other with full coffee cups, Susan opened with "Look, Wes, let's say that your story is true, then you must know many things that will happen in this war with Japan. The events happening now were historical events in your time, right? So tell me something, what is going to happen?"

"Come on, Susan. Think about what you are asking. I know that the United States wins the war, but remember, that was twenty-some years before I was born. Here today it is the tenth of December 1941. I can relate to you several events that I remember because they happened about the same time my father was taken prisoner during the German withdrawal from the Tobruk sector of North Africa. That was on the seventeenth of December 1941. That's all part of my family history. Just prior to that, Germany declared war on the US on December 11. I told you all that before, the first time. And if I remember right, two British ships will be sunk by Japanese planes today, December 10. My dad always said the luckiest thing that ever happened to him was being captured and spending the war in a prison camp. Otherwise, he might have ended up on the eastern front, fighting the Russians."

Frowning, Susan asked, "What do you mean 'fighting the Russians'?"

"My dad, right now, this day, is a tank engine mechanic with Rommel's Twenty-First Panzer Division in North Africa. He's going to be captured by the British in eight days. When Rommel pulls out of Tobruk on the eighteenth, many troops will be sent to the Russian front."

Not listening, Susan failed to notice the sudden change that had come over me. She could only think of getting to Corrigan's office to discuss what she had just uncovered. Unnoticed, I had become suddenly nervous thinking about my father and mother. I was greatly relieved when Susan started picking up her notes and called for the sentry outside. "Wes, let's wrap this up for today. We can continue tomorrow." As the sentry entered the room, I did a double take. It was the sailor I had met in the diner, Seaman Dickson, who winked but didn't say anything.

Later, sitting on my bunk, I thought back to when I was a kid. My dad told me, "Declaring war on the US was a huge mistake which destroyed the German nation." That was really firsthand knowledge. My dad and mom had been born and raised in Dortmund, Germany. Dad had been a member of the Hitler Youth Movement as a boy and had joined the German army at age seventeen, surviving the war as a POW. He was returned to his home in 1946 and married my mother in 1947. They had immigrated to the United States in 1960, two years before I was born. My father's family name of Junier had been Americanized to Jenner when they became citizens. What really twisted my shorts was that I suddenly realized my own existence was now in jeopardy in a second way: If I should say something that could be used to change the direction of the war in progress, that could change the course of the war and one or both of my parents could become a casualty. In that case, they would never meet, and I would never be born.

Thinking more about it, if anyone directing the war effort in any of the countries involved knew what was written in the history books of the future, the entire history of the world from 1942 on could be dramatically changed. I decided there was no way in hell I was going to talk about D-day or the atomic bomb. Mentally upset, I skipped dinner and slept the night through. The sound of a bugle sounding reveille brought me back to the present.

Sitting in the mess hall, I looked forward to spending time with Ms. McEuen but was bound and determined not to say anything critical. Being locked up in a cell all day was the pits. Even the guards refused to talk, other than to point out spots I missed with the mop during cleaning time. All the other people who had been sitting in the various cells were gone. I was the only one left. It was like being in solitary confinement. I thought, *I guess when the world is at war, every man is needed.*

Leaving the mess hall, Seaman Dickson escorted me back to the empty cellblock. *Damn*, I thought, *no Ms. McEuen this morning.* After seeing me to my cell and checking to be sure it was secure, Dickson hung around instead of leaving, as per the normal routine. Watching him light a smoke, I sensed that he wanted to talk, which was fine with me. I don't like sitting, doing nothing.

"What's going on, Dick? Being without a newspaper or radio is the pits."

"Well, it doesn't look good," Dick said. "Right now it sounds like we're getting the worst of it, and I've been told I'll be stationed here for a while. My division is packing up to be relocated to Hawaii—Ford Island. I hear the seaplane facility was hit pretty hard on the seventh. Hell, I'm a carpenter's mate striker. I should be with the crew, not being a babysitter. I guess I shouldn't be talking like that, but you're not going anywhere, and neither am I. Say, do you happen to play acey-deucey?"

Without even thinking, I replied, "No, I don't know the game, but I can sure learn in a hurry."

Dickson left and returned shortly with a game board and a couple of chairs. With me sitting on the edge of my bunk and playing through the bars of the cell, Dickson started to explain the game. For the next couple of days, the routine was the same: up in the morning, over to the mess hall, back to the cell, mop and clean the deck, and acey-deucey. During the course of the day, we would talk over the game board. Other times, we'd just sit and talk and drink coffee from an inexhaustible supply that Dickson had access to. I couldn't help wondering what had become of Susan McEuen but refrained from asking.

Conversation between us was stilted at first, but as time went by, things loosened up. I'm not stupid, and I know sure as shooting both Dick and Susan had been assigned to pump me for all the info they could get. I could tell they were still nonbelievers, but they were tilting in my direction because of the few things I'd told them that did come to pass. The Germany-Italy thing was the game buster.

During a lull in the game playing, Dick asked me about my schooling, job training, and working in machinery design and sales. He was blown away when I mentioned the amount of dollars in sales commissions above and beyond salaries that could be made. He couldn't appreciate or comprehend much of what I told him but concluded that I was probably good at whatever it was that I did. Over a fresh cup of coffee, Dick jokingly said, "If you're good at doing all that machinery and designing stuff, they ought to put you to work in one of the shops. I've got a buddy who complains about how bad the equipment is in the machine shop. You would be doing more good out there fixing stuff than sitting here playing acey-deucey. Then they could let me ship out and catch up with my division."

Later that evening, when I was alone, I thought about what Dick had said. Maybe at the next opportunity, I'd mention it to Susan. Nothing ventured, nothing gained. That thought led to another: *Susan, where are you?*

Across town, Susan McEuen was sitting in Jim Corrigan's office in deep conversation. "Jim, he knew what he was talking about. He said it would happen, and it did. Jim, he wasn't hedging or guessing. He knew it was going to happen."

Stopping his pacing up and down, Corrigan faced her. "Come on, Susan, that doesn't support his story. If anything, it supports him being a spy. Hell, if he was a top agent, he would know about the Germans joining the Japs, and as far as the sinking of the HMS *Prince of Wales* and the HMS *Repulse* down around Singapore, he didn't name the ships. And for that matter, the Tobruk thing still remains to be seen.

"Look, I'll admit I've got my doubts about the spy thing, but I need a lot more proof to buy that 'time traveler' story. Susan, get back to Sand Point and pump that guy. You and the sailor are doing great, but we need more data. Think about it: if he is what he says he is, he's more valuable to us than all the gold in Fort Knox. Get on it!"

FACTS ARE FACTS

'The only thing new in the world
is the history you don't know.
—Harry S. Truman, Thirty-third President
of the U.S. 1945–1953

December 16, 1941
Sand Point Naval Air Station

Leaving the mess hall on Saturday morning, Dick said, "No acey-deucey today, pal. The redhead is back and wants to talk some more." Upon entering the same old crammed office, I couldn't believe the deep feelings that struck me as I saw her standing by the window.

"Hello, Mr. Jenner. I understand you have become quite an acey-deucey player. Please sit down." Shoot, we're back to the "mister" thing again. I grabbed the chair closest to her desk and nudged it even closer, waiting for her to take the lead. Once seated, Susan shuffled through a stack of papers, looked up, and asked, "How did you know about the British ships and the Germans declaring war? What else can you tell me to support your story and dispel the impression that you are an enemy agent? Nothing you have disclosed has been verified."

Thinking about how to answer her questions, I pointed to the coffeepot on the credenza and, with her nod, got up to fill a mug.

"Can I pour you one?" She smiled and shook her head no. Returning to my chair, I sat down, holding the mug with both hands. I could feel the warmth in my palms. "Look, Susan, you are trying to get answers to things that have not yet happened. The Rommel thing won't happen for a couple more days. Likewise, you can't find a trace of the Jenner family in California. They don't get there until 1960. There's no California Machinery Company. It isn't established until 1988. Right now the ground where the company will be built is an orange grove. That's why the current location is named Orange County—lots of orange groves. Really, Susan, I can tell you many things that will come to pass. Bob Hope will become the most noted entertainer of the era for his travels to entertain troops all over the world. The Andrews Sisters will have a bunch of hit songs like 'Don't Sit under the Apple Tree' and 'Boogie Woogie Bugle Boy.' Clark Gable and Jimmy Stewart will join the Army Air Corps. Glen Ford will join the Navy. Then later, after we win this war, we will have to fight Communism in Korea and again in Vietnam, which you currently call French Indochina, until the French get kicked out by the rebels. I can tell you things that won't be guesses or predictions—they will be facts, and you can bet your life on it. But, Susan, I'm not going to talk about the war. I'm afraid to. Let me explain." With that, I opened the floodgates to all my thoughts and fears, pouring out all the things that had been on my mind and keeping me awake at night.

In this manner, the hours flew by, stopping only for short periods dictated by physical need. We forgot all else, continuing on into the late afternoon—question, answer, explanation—without either of us being aware the afternoon light faded away into darkness, as it does early in the Pacific Northwest during the winter months. I sat there exhausted, looking at Susan. I marveled at how perfect she was, wanting her and knowing it could never happen. As we sat in the waning light with nothing more to say, she stood, turned on a small desk lamp, and walked to the window to close the blackout curtains. As she stood on her toes reaching for the curtains, I couldn't help but admire her figure. Turning and aware that I had been watching her, she smiled self-consciously, leaning against the windowsill. "It's late, Wes. Let's call it a day, okay?"

Figuring it was now or never, I rose and walked to where she was standing and placed my hand on hers. "Susan, I know it's difficult, but I'm telling you the truth. Give me a chance to prove my worth. I'm a damned good engineer and tool designer. Dick was saying how they could really use someone in the machine shop with the skills I have. Keep me under guard or whatever, but let me do something other than sit in a cell. Dammit, I'm not a criminal, and I love this country as much as you do." She nodded her head, gathered her papers, and left the room. She found that she had failed to take any notes all afternoon. There was something about Wes Jenner that frightened her—not from a physical standpoint, but from a very profound emotional one. She admitted to herself that she was strongly attracted to this strange man, something she had never experienced before.

9

NOTHING VENTURED . . .

An ace in your sleeve is
worthless—unless you use it.
—"Doc" Holiday, gambler/gunfighter, 1851–1887

Susan McEuen, at age twenty-seven, had worked for the Navy Department for five years. The youngest of four children, she had been raised in a typical middle-class family—that is, until the stock market crash of 1929 wiped out the family assets. With the death of her father in 1931, followed by the loss of her mother a year later, her life changed dramatically. Taken in by an older brother and his family, she was determined to earn her own way while getting an education. She pursued this course, allowing nothing to interfere with reaching her goal. Graduating with a business degree from the University of Washington, she scored exceptionally high on a civil service exam and was selected for a position as administrative assistant at Sand Point Naval Air Station. With her first paycheck, she had found a small house for rent in the Windermere District of Seattle, within walking distance of the Naval air station. She had finally found the peace and serenity she had lost as a teenager. This fierce determination to achieve personal independence during the depth of the Depression had left little time for social play. An exceptionally pretty young lady with a shapely five-foot, four-inch frame, she easily attracted male attention. Dating occasionally, she had yet to meet someone she could seriously become involved with—until maybe just recently.

Having spent the day in the confinement of the small office talking with Wes Jenner, her little house now seemed quite spacious as she scurried around the kitchenette preparing a quick dinner, thinking aloud while peeling a potato, "Tomorrow morning when I talk with Mr. Jim Corrigan, I'll suggest what Wes talked about more freedom and a chance to work in the machine shop. Yep, help the war effort. I wonder what he'll say to that suggestion?"

The following morning, Susan related to Corrigan all that had been discussed the day before. She admitted that she was starting to believe the wild story, as strange as it was. "The reasons he states for not wanting to talk about the war are understandable. But I really think with a little more space and a little more freedom to move about, he'll talk more."

Corrigan replied, "You may be right, Susan, but think about this: If Mr. Jenner is, in fact, a visitor from the future and we are going to win the war as he says, he would be a greater asset to the enemy. His knowledge could be utilized to change the war effort in favor of our enemy. In that respect, it becomes critical that he remain in our hands even if he tells us nothing. It's more important that he reveal nothing to the enemy. You know, Susan, I don't want to say this, but for the good of the country, he would be better off dead. That would eliminate all threats."

Susan was shocked by the thought that Jim had just presented. There had to be other considerations. In her mind, she knew there had to be—for personal reasons. Quickly changing the subject, she again suggested using Wes's skills in the shop. "It doesn't make much difference if he's in a cell under guard or in the shop under guard. He can't go anywhere. You know as well as I do he's not an enemy agent. Admit it, Jim. I know you agree with me on this. The only question is where he's from and how he got here."

Putting on his coat, Corrigan nodded. "Okay, Sue, let me think about it, and I'll see what I can do."

The next morning after leaving the mess hall, I was surprised when I was led into a small machine shop. Dick was smiling. "Okay, buddy, here's your chance to prove yourself. Let's see what you can do. Some of these machine tools are still workable, but most of it is junk. That's why they shoved them over here out of the way." I spent the rest of the day dismantling old equipment, inspecting parts, and making notes. After the evening meal, and again to my surprise, I was taken to a small security apartment adjacent to the bachelor officers' quarters by the duty petty officer—a small stocky sailor who says his name is Digger.

"This is your new space, Jenner. Better than a cell. I don't know how you rate this. You may have the others faked out, but not me. I still think you're a spy, so don't try anything dumb. I'd be glad to shoot you myself." With that, he left the unit, and I heard the door bolt slide into place. It seemed that officers being held for bad conduct or whatever had better facilities than the enlisted guys. Looking around, I found that the unit consisted of a small kitchenette/dining area, a combination sleeping/living room, and God bless America, a private head and shower. Stacked on the combination bed/settee were some of my personal belongings and clothes. After a long shower and dressed in jeans and a white Tshirt, I turned on the small RCA radio sitting on the end table and listened to the news and Christmas music. I fell asleep feeling that things were going to get better.

For the next week, I spent every available hour working in the shop. That was better than sitting in the small living unit. Even the constant surveillance by the military guards became routine. Scavenging usable parts from unfit equipment as well as refurbishing others, I was able to salvage several of the larger lathes and other metalworking tools. I couldn't improve their designed capability, but I was able to greatly increase their productivity through the manufacture of various unique jigs and fixtures. My real pride and joy was the restoration of a small precision metal-turning lathe. I used this repeatedly, making small replacement parts for those that could not be salvaged or restored.

Every day Susan or Dick or both would stop by and talk while I worked on a project. Sometimes we'd all have lunch together. It was hard for me to concentrate with Susan near. I loved it when we made eye contact. She would smile and stop talking momentarily and then continue. Watching her walk across the shop was a sight to behold. The master chief aero machinist, the shop supervisor, had to be worried that her walk through the shop would result in a lost time accident as all the guys watched her walk by.

In my spare time, usually lunchtime, I had a special project going. Using a fine pencil tip torch, I was downsizing my gold signet ring. Using my small lathe, I had chamfered the edges, milled the ring surface flat, and then milled the face, leaving a small raised edge. With a stencil template, I had engraved the letter S on the face of the ring. This would be my Christmas present to Susan. I had already made a money clip for Dick using stainless steel and attaching a small crossed-anchors Navy emblem found in a workbench drawer. As it was buffed and polished, I was almost tempted to keep it for myself.

As I was taking a break in the afternoon with Dick, who had relieved the morning guard, we made small talk over a cup of coffee. I had a plan in mind, and I needed Dick to help me pull it off. "Dick, there's something I want to do, but I really need your help to do it. Help me in this, and I promise to make you a rich man. What do you say?"

"Whoa, come on, Wes. Don't ask. I think you're an okay guy and you're getting a bum deal for which you're not responsible, but don't ask me to do something illegal, okay?"

I replied, "Hold it, Dick. It's not what you think, honest. I'd like to have you and Susan to my—excuse the expression—apartment, for Christmas dinner. That's where I need your help. I was hoping you could get me some steaks, potatoes, and a few other items from your brother-in-law at the diner. I can't pay you any money. I'm broke. But I can provide you with some information with which you can make a bundle. There are some major sporting events coming up, and with the info I can give you, you can lay down some sure-thing bets and clean up, like a bandit with keys. What do you say?"

Watching his face, I could see him start to bend. "Damn, I don't know, Wes. What kinds of events are you talking about?" I knew I had him hooked. Everybody likes a sure thing.

"How about the next heavyweight fight? Joe Lewis is fighting Max Baer. I can tell you the winner and the round. Even better, I can tell you who wins the 1942 Rose Bowl and also the World Series. That one is going to be a real upset. You could bet on which teams win league pennants and then bet each game of the World Series. Dick, you could win enough to become a rich man. Dammit, man, I'm from the future. Let me prove it to you!"

Dick stood up, coffee cup in hand. "Okay, make me a shopping list, and I'll see what I can do." Grinning, I went back to work after telling Dick the score of the Rose Bowl game. Thank heaven for Sports Trivia!

Even with the security placed to protect the knowledge of my existence, my work area had become known almost overnight. This area of the shop became known and referred to as 'the Sorcerer's Work Area. Anyone who needed a small precision part made or an intricate hydraulic valve repaired made his way to this work space for help that was always provided. I soon had a backlog of work to be accomplished. The general consensus was that I was working on some secret project, to explain the constant security that surrounded me. Meanwhile, Dick and his brother-in-law at the diner were laying down bets on the upcoming Rose Bowl game. Both were a little hesitant and limited betting to the maximum amount they could afford to lose just in case my info that Oregon State would win over Duke 20–16 turned out to be bogus. This was to be the test case.

December 23, 1941
1900 hours

The small kitchen was stocked with food. Dick had really come across with his end of the bargain. Christmas Eve dinner should be a success if quantity was the criteria. Quality was the thing I worried about.

Susan had quickly agreed to be there and insisted on bringing a side dish and asked what I wanted. I had told her to surprise me. When I told her I was grilling T-bone steaks to go with loaded baked potatoes, sautéed onions, and mushrooms, she had been elated. "Wesley, that's my absolutely most favorite meal—T-bone and grilled onions."

December 24, 1941
1700 hours

I had spent almost the whole day preparing for dinner. I bounced around the small kitchenette like a ball in a pinball machine. Now, with potatoes baking in the small oven, everything was in place, and the only thing left to do was grill the steaks after everyone arrived. Yeah, sure—everyone; my guest list was two people. But it could be worse. I could still be sitting in a cell. An hour later, the security guard knocked on the door and ushered Susan into the room. Laden with packages and a decorated small tree, she smiled. "Ho, ho, ho. Something sure smells good. Come and give me a hand with this stuff."

Setting the packages on the floor with the small tree, I helped her remove her coat. Standing so close, I could detect a hint of perfume. As she turned, without thinking, I reached out and touched her cheek. "Thank you for being here. Merry Christmas, kid." Before she could respond, a second knock on the door announced Dick's arrival.

Entering and waiting until the guard closed the door, Dick reached inside his Navy peacoat and produced a bottle of champagne. "Here you are, my friends. I brought you all a present." Then, reaching in again, he pulled out three paper cups. He handed me the bottle. "Okay, Mr. Engineer, if you can open that bottle, we'll toast the holiday season."

As I opened the bottle, Dick removed his coat and helped Susan position the tree and the few small packages she had brought with her. Handing each a paper cup, I poured the wine. "Here's to better times."

"Yes," Susan said, "and to our guys in the Philippines. May God bless and protect them." That really got to me. For right now, only I knew the Philippines were a lost cause.

After drinking the toast, we all stood there, saying nothing. The fever of Susan's toast had touched a nerve in all of us. Realizing what had happened, she broke the spell and asked, "Is there anything I can do to help in the kitchen?"

I shook my head. "No way. You guys sit down, and I'll put on the steaks. I'll put your casserole in the oven also."

My meal went over without a hitch. Over after-dinner coffee, we sat and talked about past Christmas holidays during better times. The only references to the future came when I gave them each a list of stocks to invest in and important dates to remember in the years ahead. Both heaped praise upon me for the dinner, but I played it down and thanked Dick for all his efforts.

As Susan started to take the few dishes to the kitchen, I winked at Dick and handed him a pencil and a pad of paper, saying, "Write this down: Joe Louis wins by a knockout in the first round. Saint Louis beats the Yankees by winning four straight after losing the opening game. Oregon State beats Duke 20–16 in the Rose Bowl. But remember, the game will be played in Durham, North Carolina, because of the war. V-E Day will be May 8, 1945, and V-J Day will be August 15, 1945. But the formal V-J surrender will be held on the USS *Missouri* on September 2, 1945, Tokyo time. Remember, that's the truth. The Sorcerer told you. You can bet the farm on it."

Later I sat with Susan on the settee, while Dick straddled a chair. We shared stories and laughed a lot. During a lull, I stood, saying, "Listen, I really appreciate you guys coming and spending time with me tonight. I want to give you each something. It's not much but just something to express my thanks to each of you." I handed them each a small package. Susan looked at Dick.

"You open yours first, Dick. I'll open mine later." Unwrapping the gift, Dick looked at the money clip and rubbed his thumb over the Navy emblem of fouled anchors.

"Wow, this is really swell, Wes. Thanks a lot." Winking at me, he added, "I'll be able to use this in the near future." Holding out his hand, and with emotion in his voice, he said, "I like you, Wes Jenner. I wish we could have met under different conditions and at a better time." Shaking his hand, I just nodded. Picking up his peacoat, he motioned at the door. "I hate to eat and run, but I have things to do. You know, three's a crowd, and I've got the watch. Thanks again, Wes. And, Susan, Merry Christmas." After giving Susan a hug, Dick left.

I looked at Susan, holding the small wrapped gift. "It's your turn, kid. Open it, please." As she removed the ring, I took the paper. Turning the ring, she traced the engraved *S* with her index finger.

"Wes, this is such a beautiful gift. I have never received anything this beautiful before, really. But, Wes, I can't take this from you. A gold ring has so much meaning. You understand, don't you?"

As she laid the ring on the end table, I took both of her hands in mind. "Susan, listen to me. I don't know how I got here or why. I don't know how long I will be able to stay. But I know one thing for sure: I love you, Susan McEuen, and time will never change that. Please keep the ring. You don't have to wear it, but please, I want you to have it." Putting my arms around her, I buried my face in her hair and pulled her close to my body. She, too, held me tight. Never had emotion stirred two people so deeply. We stood without moving, forgetting everything, aware of only the feeling that had overcome the two of us. We kissed, then kissed again, then separated, but continued to hold hands, neither wishing to relinquish the touch of the other. Finally, Susan released my hand and removed a gold chain from around her neck. Sliding a small locket from the chain, she replaced it with the signet ring and, putting it back around her neck, let it drop inside her blouse. Watching every movement, I smiled. "Thank you."

Adjusting her blouse, she laughed. "Don't thank me, Wesley Jenner. You dropped in from heaven knows where, turned my world upside down, and made me fall in love with an alien spy who doesn't have a paying job! Find some music on that radio and let's dance."

Sand Point Naval Air Station
December 25, 1941

Christmas Day on a military base in time of war is not considered a holiday. By nine o'clock, I was in the shop, working. About an hour later, Dick walked up carrying two cups of coffee. "Okay, buddy, break time. How's it going? I thought you'd be sleeping in this morning."

"Oh yeah?" I asked. "Why's that?"

"Well, seeing as you had company 'til three in the morning, I thought you'd still be in bed."

Stopping the lathe and turning, I asked, "How the hell do you know how late I had company?"

Dick smiled, reached for his smokes, and said, "Take it easy, pal. I'm on your side, remember? Who do you think had the midwatch? I walked her out to her car."

Concurrently, across town, a different type of meeting was taking place. A small group of civilian and military personnel were gathered behind closed doors discussing implementation of the National Security Programs, or NSP, in particular those concerning the West Coast of the United States. Representatives of local, state, and federal agencies had been addressed, and action committees had been appointed. As the group was about to break and go their separate ways, Captain Anderson caught the attention of Jim Corrigan and motioned him to a corner of the room where they could talk privately.

"Jim, I haven't had the chance to get back to you concerning the man being held at Sand Point, the one picked up the day of the bombing. That one is a real puzzler. As you know, items in his possession are mind-blowers. One good thing that has been gained is the fuel injection system on that automobile—better than ours! We're updating our aircraft engines to utilize their technical expertise. Most of the other items are giving our people nightmares. Right now, the powers that be don't give a hoot if he's from Tokyo, Berlin, or Mars. It's absolutely mandatory that we learn everything this man has knowledge of. I've been directed to take you out of the loop and turn this guy over to the Army medical team at Fort Lawton. They will debrief him. I know what you're thinking. Don't ask."

Corrigan had been employed by the US government long enough to know that at times like this, you listen, keep your mouth shut, and don't ask questions. "I understand," he said.

Pausing for a moment, Anderson said, "No, I don't think you do, Jim. We are going to lose the Philippines and every soldier, sailor, and Marine out there. The Brits are in worse shape than we are. It's expected that the Japanese will have all of Southeast Asia by April '42. We can't even slow them down. What I have told you is for your ears only, understand? That's why this man's knowledge is so important. It's a given that the truth serums and drugs are experimental and may not work. In all truth, his survival is questionable. But if we can win one major battle, save a thousand men, or turn the tide of defeat in our favor, then it's worth it. As a military commander, the sacrifice of one to save many is not questionable. Jim, in the days ahead, you will have your hands full. Forget this guy. We'll touch base later." Turning, he walked away, leaving Corrigan with his thoughts.

Sunday, December 28, 1941
1630 hours

Susan had spent the morning doing her normal household chores because she had spent all day Saturday with Wes. Now she had a salmon in the oven. She planned on surprising Wes by bringing dinner to his unit so they could be together all evening. Dick had said he would be on duty that evening, drawing the "four o'clock to eight o'clock" watch. He would leave a little before eight o'clock when his relief showed up, to go see his girlfriend. She and Wes could be together all evening. Standing by the sink smiling, she thought, *This is the best job assignment I've ever had. I'm going to have to be more discreet, though. Jim Corrigan is getting suspicious.* At quarter past five, Susan, carrying everything with her, headed for the base, hoping she could park her old Model A Ford close to the main gate.

Arriving at the security unit, she was startled to find no guard on duty. Leaving her packages by the door, she walked the short distance to the security office. *Maybe he's working late in the shop*, she thought. Approaching the security desk, she was recognized immediately by the officer of the day.

"Hi, Ms. McEuen. What can we do for you this evening?"

"Hello, Lieutenant. Can you tell me where I can find Mr. Jenner?"

"Golly, Ms. McEuen, I would have thought you knew. Mr. Jenner was transferred. He was picked up early this morning. He's no longer here."

Sudden fear shook her body as the officer of the day explained how Wes was taken into custody by two civilians. "That must be some important job he's been working on."

Trying to maintain a calm she didn't feel, she asked, "Can I talk to Seaman Dickson? It's important that I meet with him."

With a shake of his head, the lieutenant replied, "That will be impossible, ma'am. Dick was shipped out this morning right after muster was taken. He hardly had time to pack his seabag. He was assigned to a destroyer scheduled for immediate deployment. I can't tell you more than that. You know, security reasons."

"Yes, I fully understand, Lieutenant. Will you please give me access to the unit Mr. Jenner had been assigned to? It's necessary for me to check several things before I go back to the office."

"I sure can. I don't see where that will hurt anything." Turning to a sailor sitting at a desk, he nodded toward the door. "Digger, go unlock the unit for the lady. Then secure it when she's through."

Following Digger back to the unit, Susan waited while he opened the door. Upon entering, she could see that the room had been completely emptied. Turning, she said, "Thanks, Digger. We can go now."

First, looking over his shoulder to make sure they were alone, Digger took a folded envelope from his jumper pocket. "Look, ma'am, I don't know what's going on, and I don't want to know, understand? Me and Dick were shipmates. We served together and looked out for one another. He asked me to be sure you got this letter. I didn't like that Jenner guy, but when your buddy is shipping out, you honor his request." Handing her the envelope, he walked out of the room ahead of her. Without further comment, she put the missive in her pocket, picked up her packages by the door, and left the area, headed for the main gate and then home.

Immediately upon entering her house and closing the door, she dropped the packages and opened the envelope. The message inside was brief and had been hastily printed on a piece of notepaper:

> Susan, this has to be quick. Wes was taken away in an army sedan.
>
> Fort Lawton, maybe. I'm being shipped out immediately.
>
> Something seems fishy. Hope you can find him.
>
> You guys were really swell. As Wes said, here's to better times.
>
> Best of luck,
> Dick

With tears in her eyes, Susan dug frantically through her purse. Finding her small address book, she noted Jim Corrigan's phone numbers, home and office. Calling both without success, she left messages to return her call regardless of the hour. As she replaced the receiver in its cradle, she looked in the mirror adjacent to the phone. "Wes, ah, Wes. Where are you? What are they doing to you? Oh, please, Lord, bring him back. Bring him back." Turning and almost stumbling, she tumbled onto the couch, buried her face in a pillow, and cried relentlessly. "Why? Why do I lose the things I love the most?"

Later in the day, without a sob left in her body, Susan stood at the stove heating water for tea when a loud knock startled her. Running to the door, she opened it to find Jim Corrigan, who pushed his way into the room. Without waiting to shut the door, she immediately attacked him verbally. "Where is Wes? Where is he? Where have they taken him? Why? Jim, I have to know. Jim, I'm in love with him. I have to help him."

Corrigan closed the door and turned to face Susan. "Look, pull yourself together, dammit. I don't know. I don't know where he is or who took him. I doubt that we will ever see him again. Susan, I'm not dumb. I've seen the change in you and Dickson too. I know of your feelings for this guy Jenner, but I didn't do anything about it, thinking the friendlier you were, the more you might learn. I've never doubted your loyalty regardless of your personal feelings. The bottom line is that powers above and beyond our levels of responsibility are calling the shots. As of right now, the past three weeks never happened. Never happened, understand?"

Without further discussion, he turned and walked out the door. After Corrigan left, she sat on the couch sobbing anew, wiping tears from her cheeks. She knew in her heart that Jim was right. The country was locked in a desperate war, and Americans everywhere were and would be facing the loss of loved ones. Maybe, with hope and prayer, who knows? In desperation, one thought gave her solace: taking the gold chain from around her neck, she removed the gold signet ring and slid it onto her finger.

Far at sea, a Navy destroyer making all possible speed pushed its bow through the swells of the North Pacific Ocean on a southwesterly course destination: Hawaii. Sitting on the mess deck, nursing a mug of hot coffee, Dick thought about the day's events and how suddenly everything took place. He hoped Digger had been able to give Susan his note. Returning to the living compartment he had been assigned to for the short transit to Pearl Harbor, he started to stow his gear in the deck locker below his bunk. He figured he might as well get comfortable.

The division's chief machinist had told him when he came on board that the ship's company was short on personnel and that he might remain on board until a replacement was assigned. As he laid his shaving kit aside, he picked up the large manila envelope they had given him as he was hustled out of Sand Point. Emptying the envelope on his bunk, he gave the contents a quick inventory: pay records, medical folder, travel orders. Closer inspection identified his destination as USN Receiving Station Honolulu, with a stateside departure date of 06 December 1941. This confirmed to one and all, if someone was to inquire, that as far as the Navy was concerned, Richard Dickson, carpenter's mate striker, left Sand Point before Pearl Harbor and could not have known anyone named Jenner.

Dick replaced the papers and locked them in his locker. As he did so, he knew that the ship's log showed him as having reported aboard the same day. End of story. There was one thing that gave him satisfaction: Reaching into his pocket, he removed the stainless-steel money clip. Holding it in his hand and rubbing the emblem with his thumb, he thought to himself, *I still have this. They can't erase everything. Now let's see how many on board this can want to bet on the Rose Bowl game.*

29 December 1941
1715 hours

After a very confusing day, I sat on a cot in an empty room waiting to see what happened next. Having been rousted out of bed in the middle of the night, I since had undergone physical exams, blood tests, and fingerprinting. Having met with total silence from the people who brought me here, I was beginning to worry about my immediate future. The room I found myself in was bare of all furniture except the cot on which I now sat. The toilet provided some privacy, being in a small alcove. The one door was an exit to the adjoining hallway. Taken to this room when I first arrived, I knew that I was in a building in an isolated area. There had been no noise of vehicular traffic or that of personnel normally associated with a military base, only the quiet efficiency of a medical facility; and that, frankly, scared the hell out of me.

Noiselessly, the door was suddenly opened, and a tall man wearing a white medical coat entered the room. Closing the door behind him, he stood looking at me and said nothing. Finally, after a long moment, he cleared his throat and spoke. "Mr. Jenner, I'm sure you are wondering what is going on and why. I have been assigned to work with you and have spent the day going over your exams and records accumulated since you have been in custody. I must say that you are one interesting individual. For your own information, you are in excellent physical condition and, much to our surprise, have all of your teeth—no fillings or gum disease. Very uncommon today for a young man of your age. I think a good night's sleep will do you good. Tomorrow we will have a busy day."

Beginning to feel a little pushed out of shape, I asked, "Just what is it 'we' will be doing tomorrow?"

"Well, you will be interviewed by a staff of individuals who have great interest in you and the circumstances surrounding your case—really nothing to worry about. It will be a long day, so I'll send something in with your evening meal that will help you sleep." With that, he turned and left the room as quietly as he had appeared.

For the first time since I was taken into custody, I experienced fear for my personal safety. "To hell with you and your busy day, my friend. I'm out of here tonight!"

Minutes later, an orderly knocked on the door and entered, pushing a cart with a tray of food and a container of milk. Pouring the milk into a glass and handing it to me, he also handed me a small paper cup holding several capsules. "Take these. They will help you sleep."

I placed the paper container on the cart, saying, "I won't need these, believe me. I can sleep like a rock without any help."

"Look, Mr. Jenner, don't be difficult. Take the pills."

I put the pills in my mouth, took a drink of milk, and started picking at my food with a fork. Seeing there were no other difficulties, the orderly left the room. As soon as the door closed, I spit the pills out of my mouth, having held them between lip and gum as I drank the milk. Quickly taking the tray of food into the alcove, I flushed it all down the toilet. "I hope there wasn't anything in the milk. They want me to go to sleep, so I guess I'd better play their game." Placing the food tray on the cart, I lay down on the cot and got comfortable. It was going to be a long night. Lying on my side facing the door with my arm over my face, I could watch the door with my face hidden from anyone entering the room. "Okay," talking to myself, I said, "now we play the waiting game."

After an interminable amount of time, I saw the door start to open slowly. From beneath my arm, I could see the legs of someone entering the room and walking quietly to where I was lying. Standing next to the cot, the person started to shake my shoulder to wake me. "Mr. Jenner? Mr. Jenner, can you hear me?" I didn't move a muscle or respond in any manner.

From outside the room, a voice asked, "Well, is he out?"

The person next to my cot answered, "Out like a light, Doctor. He won't move a muscle all night."

"Good," replied the voice in the hall. "Take the cart and dishes. Come back and check him again in an hour, before your shift is over. Be sure to tell the night desk I want him checked every couple of hours thereafter."

As the orderly left the room, he turned off the light. As soon as the door closed, I rolled over and stretched the kinks out of my back. "Now I've got a little time. Maybe I can get out of here. It must be close to eight o'clock. The orderly will be back in about an hour. Then I'll have a couple of hours to beat feet before they check on me again." With thoughts of Susan on my mind, I settled down to wait for the next bed check. Then it would be "color me gone" time. Happy New Year.

A sudden shaft of light spearing across the room brought me to full alert. Without realizing it, I had dozed off. Not moving a muscle, I feigned unconsciousness as the orderly looked into the room. Assured that I was still out, he shut the door and left. I could hear him padding away down the hall. Waiting a few minutes to allow the bed checker to get wherever he was going, I cracked the door a bit to see if it was all clear. So far, so good.

Swinging the door wider, I could see that there was no one in sight. At the end of the hallway, I could see a red 'Exit' sign shining like a beacon. Grabbing a blanket from the bed, I wrapped it around my shoulders and headed quickly down the hall. Opening the exit door, I stepped outside. The cold wind and rain quickly reminded me that it was late December in the Pacific Northwest, and the Mickey Mouse slippers they had given me to wear were already starting to soak through. Keeping my back against the side of the building, I listened for any noise that might help me out. As the cloud cover drifted and the moon was exposed, I could see that I was in a somewhat secluded area.

I waited for my eyes to become accustomed to the darkness then started to move down the side of the building toward what appeared to be a parking lot. There was no light showing anywhere, and with the overcast sky, I couldn't see a thing at first. As I got to within a few feet of the corner of the building, movement made me freeze in my tracks. As I watched, an Army sentry marched to the far end of the building and turned, marching back again. "Crap, in this darkness, I'll never get past him." Reversing direction, I started back to the opposite end of the building. Reaching the far end, I stopped to listen. Hearing and seeing nothing, I stepped around the corner, coming face-to-face with another sentry.

The sentry yelled "Halt! Halt!" while unslinging his rifle. Deciding instantly to run for it, I spun to one side to elude him. Anticipating my move, he swung his rifle butt, hitting me on the left side of my head. I fell to my knees and then into a black bottomless pit.

Thirty minutes later, in the office of the master-at-arms, both sentries stood at attention as they were questioned by the base commanding officer and the senior medical officer. "Okay, gentlemen, let's go through it one more time. Private Carter?"

Shuffling his feet, the young soldier replied, "Well, sir, I was on sentry duty at the medical complex, building 4. My assigned sector was on the north and west side, from the building to the parking lot and to the security fence. Everything was quiet and calm. Well, calm until I heard Willie—I mean, Private Williams—yelling 'Halt!' I turned on my flashlight and ran to assist him. When I got there, he was standing, holding his light on something lying on the ground. I could see it was a blanket—a hospital blanket and some muddy slippers."

Turning to look at the other young soldier, the commanding officer asked, "What happened at your post, Private Williams?"

"Sir, I also was on sentry duty at building 4. My sector included the south and east sides, from the building to the street on the south, to the security fences to the north and east. I was approaching the southeast corner of the building when, suddenly, someone stepped out directly in front of me—scared the hell out of me, sir. I yelled at him to halt, but he turned to run, so I hit him with my rifle butt, and he went down in a heap. I saw Sid—I mean, Private Carter—running in my direction. When I looked down, he, the guy, was gone. Sir, it happened in the bat of an eye. He was there, I hit him, he was on the ground, and then he was gone. Just a blanket and some slippers lying on the ground where he had dropped. That's it, sir. Honest to God, he just plain vanished!"

Shaking his head and looking at the medical officer, the commanding officer, in a disgusted voice, vented his feelings. "Dammit all, I can't believe it. The Navy—the Navy, for Christ's sake, takes this guy into custody, a person of high interest. They hold him for almost a month while letting him work in a repair shop. All this without any problems. Then we—the Army—take custody of him, and the guy disappears in less than twenty-four hours. Tell me, how do I explain that in a situation report? That sitrep will cost me a promotion, dammit—a wartime promotion! Very well, gentlemen, you're dismissed. Doctor, you stick around. I want to talk with you."

DÉJÀ VU

I'm on my way. Don't know
where, but I guess I'll get there.
—Joan Crawford, from the movie *Rain* (1932)

The sound of rain on the roof of the car and a tapping sound on the driver's side window brings me back to consciousness. Shaking my head to clear my vision causes pain to shoot across my brow. I can see that the car is sitting nose-first in a drainage ditch. More tapping causes me to turn my head slowly, and I can see to my left a Washington State Highway patrolman motioning me to open the car door. I manage to hit the door-lock release, and the patrolman opens the door and places his hand on my shoulder, telling me not to move. Seeing that I'm back among the living, he asks, "Are you in pain? Do you need assistance?"

I sense that only moments ago, the car has left the road. "Uh, I'm okay. I must have dozed off at the wheel."

Still holding my shoulder, the officer says, "You've hit your head. You didn't have your seat belt on. Do you want to sit for a moment more?"

"Nah, I'm okay. Just give me a hand." With the patrolman's assistance, I get out and stand next to my car. The cold air and slight rain combine to help clear my head. "I have an appointment in Seattle, and the freeway stopped and was all backed up, so I thought I'd try a side road. Where am I, anyway?"

"Come over to my car and sit down out of the rain," the patrol-man replies. "Right now you are on the West Valley Highway between Tukwila and Renton Junction. Let me get a little information from you. Then we'll get a tow truck to assist you."

Sitting in the waiting room of the Mercedes service department in downtown Seattle, nursing a cup of machine-made coffee, I can't help but think this trip is starting out to be a real mess. The charter-boat thing is going to cost a pretty penny. The Canadians better come through big-time. I'm going to need a big sale just so CalMac can make a marginal profit. With my headache starting to recede, I can't help but think of the dream I had while I was unconscious. Fragments of it keep popping up in my mind. The beautiful bronze-haired woman, World War II, Sand Point—what the hell was that all about? The thought of the woman—Susan, yeah, Susan. Was it McEuen? Just the thought of it makes me feel emotion that dreams just don't produce—at least not any of the ones I've had. It was all so real. Susan, Susan? I don't even know anyone named Susan. Susanne, maybe, but no one named Susan.

Catching the eye of a service attendant filling out forms at the counter, I ask, "Excuse me, could you tell me if there is a place called Sand Point near Seattle?"

"Sure, Sand Point Naval Air Station. It's just north of the University of Washington on Lake Washington. You want to know how to get there?"

"No, not really. Someone just mentioned it to me," I reply.

"Yeah, it used to be quite a naval base, but I understand they will be closing it before much longer—the Federal Base Closure Act. I guess the Navy doesn't need it any longer. Uh-oh, here comes the boss with the dope on your car."

Smiling, the service manager steps up to the counter. "All right, Mr. Jenner, it's not all that bad. You have damage to the front left suspension, tire damage and minor damage to the left front quarter panel. I estimate it at about 3,200 and change. We'll have your insurance company send out an adjuster to take a look. We can have it all done and out of the body shop before you finish in Vancouver. Give us a call before you leave Canada, okay?"

I nod to him and throw my coffee cup in the trash can. "Sounds good. Let's go for it. Can I use your phone to call a cab? I have to get out to Lake Union."

"Get your gear together, and one of our customer service drivers will take you to where you have to go," says the service manager.

"Gee, thanks. That's a time-saver. I really appreciate that," I reply. "I'll call and get the boat location and directions." As I dial the number, I notice for the first time that I'm not wearing my ring. Hmmm . . . it must be in my shaving kit. Charley had been right again. The ring was cumbersome and heavy, and I did remove it from time to time. I'd look for it later.

Arriving at the boat dock, I can see a large span of water and a bridge spanning a ship's canal. As I unload my gear, a husky young man approaches. "Mr. Jenner? We've been expecting you. I'm Carl Bryant, first mate and the skipper's go-fer. Let me give you a hand. We're down on B dock—the only boat there right now. The skipper is itching to get out of here and outrun this weather front."

Thanking the driver and grabbing the rest of my stuff, I follow the young man as he heads down the wharf where a forty-six-foot sport fisherman is moored. As I approach the boat, a woman is coiling a hose into a pier stowage locker. As she turns to greet me, I nearly step off the pier into the water. Moving to the gangway to greet me is a beautiful woman with bronze hair—an exact double of the girl in my wild dream. "Welcome aboard, Mr. Jenner. I hope you're not superstitious, but I'm the skipper of the *Signet*. My brother, Carl, and I own the boat. I'm Susan Bryant. I'm sorry you had so much trouble getting here—particularly with us asking you to arrive earlier than we had originally planned. I truly mean to make up for it, honest. Follow Carl down to your cabin and get settled in. I'd like to get underway while we still have daylight left. Get unpacked, then come topside. The transit through the government locks into Puget Sound is a kick. Hope you brought a camera." I just nod, still in a daze with what's happening. Bronze hair, green eyes, great body, and a boat named *Signet*. Déjà vu. I'm going to enjoy trying to solve this puzzle. I have to smile at the thought of it.

Following Carl forward and down the companionway, I find myself standing before a small stateroom containing a bunk and two small lockers, one on each side of the compartment. "Make yourself comfortable. Head and shower behind that door. When you get changed and come topside, bring your coat. Puget Sound can get cold. If you need deck shoes, let me know, okay?"

As I start to unpack, I feel as well as hear two diesel engines fire up and the boat come alive. I have to admit to myself this really is exciting, never having been on a boat this size before. I hope I don't get seasick and make a fool of myself.

Twenty minutes later, I'm in the galley with a cup of coffee—good coffee—in hand. Both Carl and Susan are waiting for me. "Well, Mr. Jenner, may we call you Wes?" asks Susan.

"Please do."

"Okay, then, Wes, when you finish your coffee, give Carl a hand, and we'll get the *Signet* headed for deep salt water."

I assist Carl taking in the remaining bow and stern lines then make my way forward as Susan engages the reverse gears and the *Signet* seems to shrug and then move slowly astern. Clearing the slip and using only the props, Susan brings the bow around and heads up the ship channel, passing the channel buoy. I look at Carl. He smiles and says, "She's really good. She can maneuver this baby better than a housewife can push a grocery cart. You're in good hands, Wes. She knows every inch of this boat—every system, piping, electrical—all of it. She was taught by our grandmother—if you are going to do something, don't screw around, do it right. Don't fuss and think it to death. Just do it. That's my big sister."

Getting out of the light rain, I climb to the enclosed bridge area and stand behind Susan as she maneuvers the *Signet* up the Lake Washington ship canal headed for the Ballard Locks. She explains that we are still in fresh water and won't enter the salt water of Puget Sound until we pass through the locks.

Officially opened in 1917, the Ballard Locks were constructed to allow boat traffic to move from the fresh water of Lake Washington and Lake Union into the salt water of Puget Sound while preventing the mixing of seawater with that of the freshwater lakes. We enter the smaller of the two locks with four other private boats and one large tugboat. Approximately thirty minutes later, we've dropped about twenty feet to sea level and are cruising through Shilshole Bay headed for points north.

Once clear of the boat traffic around the locks and headed north into Puget Sound, Carl takes over the helm, allowing Susan and me to become acquainted and talk. She motions out through the glass panels at the light rain and says, "The weather in May is very unpredictable here, but we should be able to soon leave it behind us. The front is moving from the northwest and headed south. The *Signet* is a very comfortable boat, so make yourself at home, please. All we really understand from our previous planning is that you want to go salmon fishing."

Looking at Susan as she talks, I can't help but notice that when she is talking and makes eye contact with me, she smiles, stops talking momentarily, and then continues. It seems like a case of more déjà vu. Snapping out of my reverie, I answer, "Well, Susan, to be honest, I've never been fishing before. I really needed a long vacation, but that's a different story, so I figured I'd combine the two and made contact with you. I really picked winners with you and Carl. You two will have a real greenhorn on board."

Unrolling a chart of the Puget Sound across the navigation table, she starts to make suggestions. Pointing to a spot on the map, she says, "This is Bainbridge Island." Then, pointing out to the portside, she says, "That's it there. The marker is Monroe Point. We can overnight in Port Townsend then make our way north and play around the San Juan Islands for fishing. We'll have to stay in American waters. We aren't licensed to fish Canadian waters, but we could go north as far as the Campbell River to see the country. It's your call."

As she talks and becomes engrossed in planning our coming days, I can see more and more of Susan McEuen in her mannerisms. Is it my imagination? "Susan, I'm putting myself in your hands. Let's catch some salmon, and then we'll play it by ear."

"You know, Wes, Carl and I have never—and I mean never—had a company charter of this duration with only one other person aboard. I don't have to tell you what it means to us. We really needed a charter, but this one is a dream charter. With only the three of us on board, it's a vacation for all of us." The two of us just sit there saying nothing more. The muted but throaty sound of the diesel engines, coupled with the motion of the craft breasting the swells, has a narcotic effect on me. Watching a ferryboat cross our wake well astern of us, I can't help thinking that for a day that started out so crappy, I've never felt so content.

"Would you like to go up to the open bridge area?" Susan's voice brings me out of my reverie.

"Well, I was really thinking about going down and getting some shut-eye."

"That's a good idea," she says. "You look like you could use some sleep. Go below and sack out. When we get moored, Carl will wake you, and we'll see about dinner."

I wake slowly from a deep, dreamless sleep. The boat is quiet except for the slight sound of water lapping against the side of the hull. I can feel a soft bump as the hull meets with something solid. Looking at the illuminated dial of my watch, I can see it's a little after 10:00 p.m. Rolling off the bunk, I dress quickly, make an urgent head call, spending extra minutes trying to figure out what valve to turn and what lever to pull to make the toilet flush. Washing with cold water brings me to full awake, chasing all sleep from my mind. Looking through the glass port above my bunk, I can see that we are side-tied to another boat. Making my way aft, I can hear music wafting softly from the intercom. Entering the salon, I find Susan in conversation with an older couple.

"Well, welcome back to the land of the living. I was beginning to worry about you," she says. "Wes, meet Rick and Janet Ekstrom. They own and operate the Grand Banks *Apollo* that we are side-tied to. They have a charter going north also. We are both leaving in the morning, so we'll have company near at hand. If you are hungry, there's salmon, wild rice, scalloped potatoes, and salad in the galley. Help yourself."

As I eat, I listen to Susan relate to the Ekstroms the problems I encountered coming north. Having finished a second helping, I settle down with a cold can of Rainier and join the conversation. A short time later, the Ekstroms return to the *Apollo*, leaving the two of us alone. "Come on, sleeping beauty. Help me square the galley away so we'll be in good shape in the morning. Eggs, bacon, and hash browns for breakfast. That's the menu whenever Carl cooks breakfast."

With that piece of information, I get up, follow Susan to the galley, and wipe dishes as she washes and hands them to me. Afterward we sit, relax, and talk. She asks me about life in Southern California. I skirt around the best I can. I'm ashamed to admit that I don't have a life, only a job. As the brass clock mounted on the bulkhead chimes midnight, Carl comes aboard and makes his way to the salon where we are sitting. With his arms full of packages, he smiles at me and says, "Wow, I'm glad to see you up and about. I was worried you died and we would have to bury you at sea."

Looking at his sister, he nods at the bags he's holding and says, "The last-minute goodies. That's it, sis. Fuel and water tanks are topped off, and we're okay to go. I don't know about you two, but I'm hitting the sack. Five o'clock comes around real quick. When you get up, Wes, wear warm clothes. It will be chilly." He turns and heads down the passageway.

Standing, Susan yawns and says, "Me too. Are you going to be able to get back to sleep?"

"Hey, with the boat rocking gentle-like, I'll sleep like a baby, believe me." With that, I end my first day aboard the *Signet*. Later, lying in my bunk, I can't get Susan Bryant, née McEuen, out of my head.

Unknown to me, in the next stateroom aft, Susan Bryant is also lying in her bunk thinking, *There's something about this Wes Jenner that seems so familiar. He stirs up my emotions, in a good way. I don't know why, but something tells me this cruise will be very different.*

Susan Rae Bryant, age twenty-seven, was born and raised in the Seattle area. She and her younger brother, Carl, spent their childhood on the waters of Puget Sound. Both she and Carl were raised by their grandparents, Susan and Jim Corrigan. Their parents had died as the result of a traffic accident. Returning from a skiing weekend on Mount Rainier, their car had skidded off the road, leaving three-yearold Susan and one-year-old Carl in the responsible hands of their grandparents. As teenagers, both Susan and Carl had rejected any suggestion of college made by their grandparents. Susan opted for seamanship and celestial navigation courses sponsored by the US Coast Guard, while Carl made a name for himself doing boat repairs in the local marinas. Their grandparents, Susan and Jim Corrigan, both retired government employees, had purchased an old thirty-two-foot cabin cruiser on which summers were spent exploring the back bays of Puget Sound, Hood's Canal, and the San Juan Islands.

As they had never known their parents, a close family bond was established among Susan, Carl, and their grandparents. Susan had an exceptionally close bond to her grandmother, whom she had been named after. This bond had instilled a spirit of adventure and self-reliance in the granddaughter, which became a family truism. "Hell," Jim used to say about his granddaughter, "the kid thinks, acts, and responds just like her grandmother. One can start to say something, and the other can finish the thought."

In the spring of 1986, after forty-three years of marriage, Jim Corrigan passed away peacefully in his sleep. His wife followed him a year later. The loss of their grandparents was the greatest Susan and Carl Bryant had ever experienced. The two were now on their own, with no backup to rely on. Taking stock of what they had and what they were capable of doing, they utilized funds inherited from their grandparents' estate and bought the *Signet*. Not a pleasure boat outfitted for fishing, the *Signet* was designed and built by a boat yard in Tacoma noted for their design and craftsmanship. The hull was of a sleek, deep V design, planked with Port Orford cedar fastened with silicon bronze fastenings. Powered by two Detroit diesel engines, this was truly a fast and dry boat, built specifically for sportfishing the waters of the Pacific Northwest while providing all the creature comforts of a yacht.

Upon completion of construction, Susan and Carl had her fitted out and equipped for charter service. Licensed and Coast Guard inspected, they were ready for business; however, charter-boat business had been hit-and-miss and over the past two years, and both had reason to question their investment as competition was keen and charters not that plentiful. Fortunately, the siblings were well versed and highly capable in boat repair and maintenance, augmenting their charter income by caretaking boats that owners rarely used except to stay aboard on summer weekends, never leaving the pier. Wes Jenner was a welcome charter. Single-party charters for multiweek periods were few and far between.

The muffled cough of the *Signet*'s small diesel generator brings me awake with a start. Grabbing a quick shower and shave, I make my way topside just as the *Apollo* backs slowly away from the pier. Simultaneously, the whine of the first Jimmy diesel comes to life aboard the *Signet*, followed shortly by the second. Damn, salt air and diesel smoke—this is exciting. Spotting Susan on the pier, I move to the rail and wave. "Anything I can do?"

Looping the bowline around a cleat, she throws the bitter end of the line to me. "Hold her snug until Carl tells you to take it in. Then just flip it loose from the cleat and haul it in, okay?"

After coiling up the shore power lead, Susan jumps from the pier to the boat, stows the lead in the gear locker, and waves to Carl, who then waves to me. "Okay, Wes, bring it in." Just like clockwork, the *Signet* slowly backs away from the pier. Again using only the props, one astern and one ahead, Carl brings the bow around and then heads for deep water. Following Susan, I make my way up to the open flybridge. Settling into a helm seat, I watch as Carl maneuvers through a multitude of commercial craft and pleasure boats dotting the screen of both the long- and short-range radar repeaters. Clearing the bulk of the boat traffic, Carl advances the throttles, and the *Signet* immediately responds. Rising and falling with the swells, the boat comes alive and begins to close on the *Apollo* a short distance ahead. Susan is busy checking the complex of shipboard monitoring systems, ensuring that all support systems are operating properly.

Over the next few days, I become familiar with the boat and begin to feel more at ease. I even take a turn at the helm to spell Carl or Susan from time to time. Arriving at the planned fishing location, there are several other boats mooching the same area. Carl teaches me how to plug-cut the frozen herring used for bait. I lose my first three hookups due to inexperience, but with constant advice from the crew, I land my first salmon—a twenty-pound king. With all the yelling and shouting, I don't know who's the most excited—the student or the teachers. Wow, I'm a convert. This is the greatest ever.

With each passing day, the amount paid for this experience is worth every red cent. In this manner, each day blends into the next, bonding the three of us together into an easy, enjoyable routine. On occasion, Susan and I pack a lunch and take off in the Boston whaler to go exploring or beachcombing. I can't get enough of the beachcombing. Washington beaches are so different from the California beaches: cold, clear water. You can actually see the bottom twenty feet or so below the boat. Steep, rocky beaches and lots of driftwood and flotsam for beach fires. I think I've found my place in the world.

Having finished a day of fishing and exploring, the *Signet* lies at anchor in a protected small cove. Tall cliffs rise from the rock-strewn beach, and tall trees ring the cliff tops. It's quiet. I have never in my life experienced quiet like this. Back on the stern, Carl sits with a line in the water, mooching for bottom fish. In the galley, I help do the evening dishes. I comment to Susan, "This has been the best thing I've ever experienced. You and Carl have made this so much more than just a fishing trip. It's really been a blast. I can't tell you how much I appreciate my time on board the *Signet*."

Susan stops what she's doing and, without looking at me, replies, "Wesley, you may have chartered this trip, but let me tell you, it has been more than just a charter to Carl and me." Turning to look at me with eyes the color of jade, she smiles, hesitates, and then says, "It's been a very special trip for me." Realizing the intensity of her comment, she says, "Come on, grab a couple of cool ones, and we'll go see if Carl's having any luck."

Late that night, the boat is really quiet except for the muted chugging of the auxiliary power generator and the soft sound of water lapping against the hull. Unable to sleep, I quietly don my leather jacket over my PJs and make my way up to the afterdeck. In the darkness, the masthead anchor light of a sailboat lying at anchor farther down the cove shimmers across the water. I stand at the rail and gaze at the night sky. Having been raised in a city lit by thousands of night lights, I've never really experienced total darkness compromised only by stars that appear as big as basketballs. Totally awed, I'm startled by a soft voice behind me. "Beautiful, isn't it?"

Turning, I see her, blanket around her shoulders, watching me. "Wow, you kind of startled me. How long have you been standing there?"

"Not long. Five minutes or so. Would you like a cup of coffee or something?"

"No, I don't think so. You know, I tried to be quiet. I sure didn't mean to wake you, but I'm glad I can share this with someone . . . with you."

She stands silently for a moment and then says, "I was awake, and I knew someone was up and about. I hoped it was you." Moving to a large padded deck lounge, she sits and says, "Come, let's sit for a while. It's so peaceful and still, isn't it? I often do this—come up on deck at night." We sit there, content, both aware of the other. I don't want to go to Vancouver. I don't want this trip to end. Then, without realizing why, I start to talk. The words just pour out—everything: my job, my broken marriage, the uncertain future, everything, but not my dream of her. Or was it her?

Having talked myself out, I just sit there, suddenly aware that I have my arm about her shoulder and we are sharing the blanket she brought with her when she first came on deck. Susan lays her head into the crook of my arm, looking at the stars overhead. Turning to me, she says softly, "I had planned to be married next month. Ron Stone. We've known each other for years. He works for Boeing and may be transferred to Wichita. It seemed right at the time that he asked me, but the more I thought about it—well,

I gave him the ring back. I can see myself still doing what I'm doing now for years. Had I married Ron, I would have become a middle-America housewife concerned about kids, home, and cooking. That's what he wanted. But to be perfectly honest, I want something different. My grandmother always told me that when the right guy came along, I'd know it and not to let common sense interfere. It made sense to marry Ronald, and that's probably why I broke the engagement."

Pulling the blanket tighter around our shoulders, she continues. "I was very close to my grandmother. She was the major influence in my life, but yet she was very secretive about her life. I know my grandfather thought she could do no wrong, and I know she loved him also, but I've always felt she had truly loved someone—someone special—before she married Granddad. I think maybe someone who was killed in the war. She always made reference to someone she called the Sorcerer. Whenever she did something she didn't want to explain, she would say the Sorcerer told her to do it. She invested in certain stocks, like Boeing, Revlon, IBM, and Clorox. She said the Sorcerer said to do it, so she did. Granddad loved her and never once argued with her about it."

I try not to laugh, thinking to myself, *I told her Xerox, not Clorox.*

But Susan pokes me and says, "Don't laugh, my friend. When she and Granddad bought their old boat, it was her investment money that paid for it. That's why they named it *The Sorcerer.* As kids, Carl and I spent more time on that old boat than anywhere else. She was slow, but she was durable. Carl and Granddad kept her in fine shape. I used to lie on the deckhouse with Grandma and sunbathe. She was my favorite person, and just as sure as we're sitting here, I feel that in some unknown way, she's still here influencing what I do." Again, we sit there, feeling the emotion suddenly brought to the surface by her reminiscing. Then, in a quiet voice, she asks, "What are you going to do after you finish in Vancouver?"

Caught off guard by the question, I take several moments to respond. "I don't know. I have mixed emotions about the whole thing, but I owe it to my boss to give it my best shot. I'll finish what

I've set out to do and then decide. What about you? Are you going to run a charter service all your life?"

"Well, Wes, I was born and raised in the Pacific Northwest, and I love boats and the water. Carl and I have often talked about someday when we can afford it buying a small boat marina and repair facility. Heaven knows, there are lots of boats around and lots of boat owners who don't know stem from stern. We'll see. Listen, we still have another day ahead of us. How about crab omelets for breakfast?"

It's then that I kiss her, then again and she kisses me back. We hold each other for a short while. Then, as quietly as she had first appeared, she goes below.

Moored at a guest pier in the boat harbor, Carl is lugging my gear up the gangway to a waiting taxi while I try to say goodbye to Susan. "Well, skipper, it's been one great adventure. I'm sorry it's over." I've shaken her hand, but I can't release it. "You and Carl made it a great trip for me. I can't say thank you enough. Would you consider having dinner with me when I get back to Seattle? Please, I really want to see you." Susan doesn't say anything, but she smiles and nods yes.

"There's something else I always wanted to ask but didn't. I'm going to ask it now, why did you name this boat the *Signet* instead of the *Sorcerer II* after your grandparents' boat?"

"We thought about it, but somehow it just didn't seem right, so we named it after Grandma's most precious possession." Removing her hand from mine, she reaches under the collar of her sea jacket and lifts a small object suspended on a gold chain from around her neck. In her hand, edges worn smooth by time, lies a gold signet ring. I can see that the engraved *S* is still prominent on its recessed bezel where I had engraved it. With the ring in her hand, she smiles in a small way that breaks my heart. "Call me, Wes. Call me, okay?"

This time, it's my turn. I can only smile and nod yes.

* * * * *

Two weeks later, I'm sitting on the upper deck of a Seattle-bound ferry. There are quicker ways to get to Seattle, but I need lots of time to lick my wounds. The past two weeks have not gone according to plan. CalMac's boy wonder has fallen on his sword, but it wasn't a complete flop. Several subsidiaries have purchased some of our standard metalworking equipment, but sales like that could have been done over the phone from our California office. Even Charley, who had flown up when he heard how the deal was going, admitted it was a lost cause. The Canadians have more of a problem than CalMac can cure.

Picking up a *Seattle Times* newspaper, I automatically turn to the business section. On the second page is a picture of five men in white hardhats pushing shovels into the ground. The caption reads, "Valley Construction Groundbreaking Ceremony." It's for a new aerospace facility to be erected in the Kent Valley. I study the picture for a moment then fold the newspaper and lay it back on the adjacent chair. Standing, I leave my seat to go and find a cup of hot coffee.

Early the next morning, having completed the paperwork and paid the deductible on my car, I leave the Mercedes dealership and head for downtown Seattle. Finding a parking garage, I leave the Benz and walk two blocks to a large office building. Taking the elevator to the twenty-first floor, I enter the lobby of the offices of Valley Construction Company. Approaching the reception desk, I'm greeted by a young blond whose smile is so dazzling it takes my breath away. "Good morning. May I help you?"

Trying to match her smile with my own, I say, "Yes, good morning. May I please speak with the president of your company?"

With a questioning look, she checks her desk day schedule and asks, "Do you have an appointment? His day is already booked. He's extremely busy at the present time."

Edging closer to her desk, I give her what I hope is my most sincere look and ask, "Please just tell him that the Sorcerer wishes to speak to him."

Standing and hitting me again with that dazzling smile, she says, "This is against my better judgment, but wait one moment, please." As she walks away, I can see that her shape is even better than her smile. In a few short moments, she returns still smiling and says,

"Please follow me." Leading me down a hallway with large hanging pictures of construction projects in various stages of completion, she ushers me into a well-appointed office with huge windows overlooking the Seattle waterfront.

Standing next to his desk is an elderly man with a shock of white hair and a big smile. I'm overwhelmed seeing him. I swallow and say, "Hello, Dick." Stepping away from his desk and walking toward me, he speaks in an old familiar voice, "Hello, Wes. It's been a long, long time, but I've been expecting you." He nods toward a window where a table and two chairs have been placed. On the table are an acey-deucey board and two old Navy coffee mugs.

Much later that same day, following directions penciled on a sheet of memo paper, I make my way to the Pike's Place Market and have a salmon shipped to Carrie then drive to the Lake Union marina where the *Signet* should be moored. Parking my car in an empty slot, I turn and head for B dock. I hear my name called loudly. Turning, I see Carl Bryant making his way through the parking lot in my direction.

Grinning from ear to ear, he greets me. "Hey, Wes. Gee, buddy, it's really good to see you." He shakes my hand and slaps my shoulder. "Listen, we just got in from a half-day charter. Sue's down on the boat, but watch your step, she's been a bear for the past two weeks. Listen, I've got to run some errands, but don't go away, okay? I'll see you later." With a wave, he gets into an old pickup truck and is gone.

Stopping at the head of the ramp, I can see Susan hosing down the boat. Watching her makes my world all right once again. That hollow feeling that has plagued me for the past two weeks is abating like an outgoing tide. As I start down the ramp, she spots me and waves. Turning off the hose, she waits for me as I approach the boat. "Well, hello there, stranger. How was Vancouver?"

"Well, not the best trip I've ever made. They treated me like the ugly American."

"Oh, I'm really sorry to hear it didn't work out well for you, but tell me something, do they have telephones in Canada?"

Man, that was a shot I hadn't expected. Abashed, I start to explain. "Susan, I was—"

She stops me midsentence. "Wes, I was just kidding, honest. Come on, let's go aboard and have some coffee." She stows away the hose, and I follow her aboard. I can't help but notice that, without a doubt, she has the blond in Dick's office beat, hands down.

Sitting in the galley with coffee poured, she looks me in the eye and says, "So Vancouver went down the pooper, but you were able to get your car out of hock. What now?"

Shrugging my shoulders, I respond, "Well, I don't know for sure. I met an old dear friend today, and we talked about the past and about the days ahead. You will really have to meet him. He knew your grandparents. He said he'll back me in anything I want to do if I plan on staying in the Seattle area. So . . . would you and Carl be interested in one more deckhand? Or how about a marina?"

Susan turns to the galley sink and picks up a dishcloth to mop up the coffee spilled when she dropped her cup. Wiping up coffee and with a straight face, she asks, "You quit your job?"

"Yep, I sure did.

Still with a straight face, she says, "And you're not going back?"

"Nope, I'm not going back. I really wish you would consider what I just asked you. I really need a job. If it would help matters, I'm also madly in love with you."

Throwing her arms around my neck, laughing and half crying, she asks, "Can you tie a square knot?"

"No, but you can teach me."

"Do you know a stem from a stern?"

"No, but you can show me." Taking her by the hand, I lead her off the boat and up the pier.

"Where are you taking me?" she asks.

"First, we're going to find Carl and get his okay for me to marry his sister. Then we'll work out all the miscellaneous stuff. Now, for you personally, if you answer some questions right, you can still be a June bride."

Releasing my hand, she stops and puts her arms around me, holding me tightly. "Even if you didn't call me, I love you, Wesley Jenner, with all my heart, and I know if she were here, Grandma would love you also and say to me, 'Go for it, kid.'"

"She's here, babe," I whisper. "She's right here."

Releasing me from her bear hug, she slips her arm through mine and asks, "Okay, Wesley Jenner. Tell me, are you taking me and Carl to dinner tonight?"

"Absolutely. Black Angus. T-bone steak, sautéed onions, mushrooms, and loaded baked potatoes."

Stopping in her tracks, she turns to me and exclaims, "How did you know? How did you know? That is my most favorite dinner!"

With a straight face, I reply, "Susan, my dear, I knew it for a fact. I could have bet money on it and given odds. The Sorcerer told me."

11

EPILOGUE

If opportunity doesn't
knock, build a door.
—Milton Berle, comedian (1908–2002)

Seattle, Washington
One year later

Driving toward the Lake Washington boat canal on Aurora Avenue, the following sign is highly visible to vehicular traffic:

JENNERS
SNUG HARBOR MARINA

FOOD – FUEL – BOAT REPAIRS
BOAT RAMP AND BOAT LIFT
SMALL-BOAT RENTALS
COVERED SLIPS AVAILABLE
CHARTER-BOAT SERVICE

TURN AT NEXT RIGHT

A very nice, full-service marina. I know, for my company built it—a company started with funding from wagers won that Oregon

State would beat Duke 20–16 in the 1942 Rose Bowl game held in Durham, North Carolina.

Richard L. Dickson, President
Valley Construction

ABOUT THE AUTHOR

Ben Swenson has written many short stories and poems, but *The Signet* is his first published work. His other writings are life experiences of the Depression years and growing up from a boy to adulthood. At age eighteen, he left the farm environment of Western Washington State and joined the US Navy. Thirty-six years later, he retired from the civilian position of planning officer for the supervisor of shipbuilding USN, Long Beach, California. He and his wife, Joyce Swenson, have two daughters, seven grandchildren, and nine great-grandchildren and live in Temecula, California.

CPSIA information can be obtained
at www.ICGtesting.com
Printed in the USA
FSHW011945240519
58453FS